Murder a

Copyright

Copyright © 2025 by Andi Cane
All rights reserved.
No portion of this book may be reproduced in any form without written permission from the publisher or author, except as permitted by U.S. copyright law.

TABLE OF CONTENTS

The Morning After	4
Footprints in the Alley	8
The Index Code	15
Councilwoman on Camera	20
The Curator Vanishes	24
Bitter Evidence	32
The Map Below	37
A Whistle and a Warning	43
Breaking the Silence	48
The Dictaphone	55
Ashes Before Dawn	60
The Fire Beneath the Glass	65
The Man Who Vanished Twice	70
Echoes in Silver	75
The Tower Files	79
Truth on the Clock	84
Where Clocks Forget	87
The River Knows	91
The Confession in the Fog	95
The Quiet After the Storm	100
Brewed Awakening	103

The Morning After

Hattie was halfway through tugging her hair into a loose knot when a pulse of blue light flickered across her ceiling. At first she thought it was the old neon sign from the bakery two doors down misbehaving again, but the second flash—red this time—soaked the walls, threading through the early hush of Maplewood Square.

She crossed the loft and pushed aside the curtain. From her apartment window above Brewed Awakening, she saw the scene clearly now: police cruisers angled across the museum's steps, an ambulance idling with its lights spinning silently, and strips of yellow crime-scene tape stretched from railing to railing. Fog clung low, making the lights reflect off the pavement

The banners from last night's Heritage Gala still hung from the columns, their silver lettering catching the emergency glow. What had looked festive twelve hours ago now looked garish and misplaced. The museum had been dressed for a celebration and woken to a tragedy instead.

Beans hopped onto the windowsill, golden tail flicking with irritation at the intrusion of noise.

"Yeah," Hattie murmured, "I'm not sure what's going on either."

Curiosity tugged at her before reason could. She fed Beans, grabbed her apron, shoved her notebook into her pocket, and headed downstairs to start her shift—and, apparently, to figure out what sort of chaos the museum had brewed up overnight.

On the sidewalk, the morning air hit her with damp chill. A small group of bystanders clustered near the cordon, whispering behind scarves and coffee cups. As Hattie approached, two paramedics emerged from the museum doors, guiding a stretcher covered completely by a white sheet. One of the museum's custodial staff—a young man who regularly ordered decaf and never made eye contact—pressed a trembling hand to his forehead. "It's Owen," he muttered to no one in particular. "Owen Pike… head of security."

"He's gone," someone else whispered back.

Hattie stopped short. She knew Owen Pike mostly by the way he snapped at volunteers and complained about paying full price for drip coffee. He had a reputation for cutting corners, hoarding authority, and rubbing absolutely everyone the wrong way.

And from the faces around her—grim, tight-lipped, not quite shocked—she could tell Maplewood had known him the same way.

Hattie's curiosity was triggered. Whatever had happened inside that museum wasn't just unfortunate—it was something Maplewood may have quietly feared, expected, or even predicted.

Inside Brewed Awakening, the warmth hit Hattie in a comforting wave—rich espresso, toasted almond, and a faint citrus scent from the orange zest. It felt soothing, normal, familiar… everything the scene across the square wasn't. She slipped behind the counter and took in the early birds already camped at tables: laptop warriors, remote workers with oversized headphones, a grad student typing furiously as if the fate of Maplewood depended on her thesis due at noon.

Some had moved on acting unaware that a body had just been wheeled out of the museum thirty yards away.

Her staff—Marcy and Josh—were already in full shot mode, though the usual chatter had been replaced by whispers and wide eyes. As Hattie passed the pastry case, Marcy leaned in without breaking rhythm on her muffin arrangement.

"You won't believe what we heard," she murmured.

"I probably will," Hattie said, but that didn't stop her from listening.

Josh wiped down tables with uncharacteristic determination. "Pike was still there after the gala ended," he said under his breath. "Like, way after. Lights on until after midnight."

"Someone heard shouting," Marcy added. "Near the loading dock. Volunteers aren't supposed to go out that way, but Margaret, the lady from Archives said she saw a shadow storm out the side door."

Hattie paused, hand resting on the pastry tongs. "A shadow?"

Marcy shrugged. "Tall. Fast. Angry."

Josh shuddered. "Pike always made people angry. Think of the way he talked to volunteers. Or the interns. Or… everyone."

Hattie tucked each detail into that quiet, careful place in her mind where theories began forming long before she admitted she saw them. She didn't want to speculate—not yet. But the picture assembling itself wasn't complicated: Owen Pike had spent years, posturing, and pressuring people. He had… collected resentment. Layer by layer. Person by person.

And the museum across the street suddenly felt less like a respectable landmark and more like a building hiding something much older and much darker.

The bell over the café door began jingling nonstop. Maplewood was awake, caffeinating, and—true to form—eager for proximity to chaos. Inside the coffee shop, regulars continued filtering to their unofficial assigned seats. Mrs. Baker and her knitting needles took a corner table. The retired mailman, who never broke his routine of one black coffee and two crossword puzzles, pretended not to stare at the police cordon through the window. A pair of high school teachers leaned close over their lattes, whispering with the urgency of people grading the mystery as if it were a pop quiz.

Mabel Cho arrived in a burst of cold air and determination, arms stuffed with newspapers and her tote crammed full of rumor-ready supplies. She slapped the morning edition onto the counter with theatrical flair.

"Someone finally snapped," she declared to no one and everyone.

The room paused. It always paused when Mabel spoke like she was narrating a radio drama.

"Mabel," Hattie warned gently and with a joking smile, "nobody even knows what happened and I didn't realize people still read newspapers."

"Oh please." Mabel accepted her caramel latte with an appreciative hum. "Owen Pike made enemies out of half this town. Would you like a list? Because I brought a pen."

Before Hattie could respond, the door opened again. This time, a familiar swish of tailored wool swept in. Councilwoman Dolores Grant positioned herself in the center of the café like a spotlight had been cued.

"What a terrible morning for Maplewood," Grant announced, modulating her voice exactly like she did on campaign stages. "We on the council wish to assure the public that we will cooperate fully with investigators."

Mabel sipped loudly. "Translation: Not our fault."

Grant's smile tightened. "This tragedy—whatever its cause—must not overshadow the Gala's success or the museum's important restoration work."

Someone mumbled, "Or the funding that keeps disappearing?"

Grant stiffened but pretended not to hear.

Hattie made her a black coffee, and as requested, three saccharine packs, no sentiment. "Rough day," she said neutrally.

"Maplewood is resilient," Grant replied, which didn't answer anything and never had.

The bell chimed again. This time Greg Benson from ZenBean Buzz poked his head in, smirking like a man who'd practiced the expression in the mirror.

"Heard you've got front-row seats to the crime of the year," Greg said. "Hope it doesn't slow business. People get jittery around police tape."

Hattie smiled tightly. "Funny. Your shop is farther from the scene. You must be devastated."

Greg sniffed, lifting his chin. "I thrive under pressure." He paused, then added with a conspiratorial wink, "You know who didn't? Pike."

"Nope," Hattie said, already moving on. "Door's behind you. Don't let it hit you on the way out."

Greg left in a puff of overpriced cologne.

As if summoned by fate, or habit, Liam arrived just in time for the peak chaos. His hair stuck up at the back, his glasses slid slightly down his nose, and he carried his laptop bag like a man ready for battle despite wearing mismatched socks. He gave Hattie a grin that softened his whole face.

"Big morning," he said as he slipped behind the counter, moving with the ease of someone who had unofficial employee status.

"You have no idea," Hattie replied.

"Oh, I have ideas." He started repairing the receipt printer before she even asked. "I walked behind two women arguing whether Pike was murdered or abducted by art thieves."

"Murdered," Mabel called from her table. "Definitely murdered."

Hattie shot her a look. Mabel sipped primly.

Liam dropped his voice. "On my walk over, I heard someone say Pike had been threatening to 'expose the board.' And another guy said Pike told him the museum's finances were a 'powder keg.'"

Hattie exhaled slowly. "He wasn't popular."

"He wasn't safe," Liam corrected.

Together they glanced out the window toward the museum where the police tape fluttered like an accusation no one was ready to voice.

Between the gossip, the rumors, the sharp edges of Pike's reputation, and the hush that settled every time the museum came into view, a single truth gnawed at the edges of Hattie's thoughts:

He didn't just die by natural causes.

Someone had a reason.

And Maplewood already knew it.

In the swirl of speculation, coffee steam, and quiet dread, Hattie felt the first unmistakable tug of a mystery forming—one that, whether she liked it or not, had already pulled her in.

Footprints in the Alley

By nine, the museum's blue-and-red pulse had settled into a steadier hum, the kind of official rhythm that says: this will take all day. The square had filled with cordons, cones, and camera crews. Brewed Awakening filled with Maplewood—teachers with backpacks, a contractor in dusty boots, retirees in windbreakers, all of them wanting caffeine and answers in that order.

I didn't have answers. I had espresso and a knot between my shoulder blades.

Sam arrived, cardigan buttoned wrong in her hurry, cheeks pink from the chill. She slipped behind the counter without a word, pulled a tray of blueberry scones from the warmer, and started plating them like she could control the universe with pastries.

"You saw the tape?" I asked.

She nodded, eyes flicking to the museum through the front windows. "I heard about Pike. And the medallion. Are we—" Her gaze dropped to the sandwich bag I'd tucked beneath the register. The staff wristband. "Hattie."

"I didn't cross anything. It was in the cracks by our dumpster. I used a lid like a scoop." I offered the bag for inspection and promptly felt like a child showing a frog in class.

"Hattie," she said again, more softly. "We run a coffee shop. Not a forensics lab."

"I know." The knot pulled tighter. "But if a staffer exited through the alley, that matters. And the river mud on it—"

"Please tell me you didn't smell it."

"By accident," I lied.

Sam folded her arms. "Promise me you'll be careful."

"Always." I reached for a towel and pretended not to notice that my definition of careful and hers were cousins who didn't speak.

Liam slid a repaired receipt printer into place with a triumphant click. "I have bestowed modern civilization upon your counter."

"Bless you," I said, then lowered my voice. "I'd like a closer look at the alley. From our side of the tape, obviously."

He glanced toward the square, then back at me. He bit his lip, the way he does when he's about to agree to something that scares him. "Five minutes. We photograph, we don't touch, we don't die. Deal?"

"Deal." I untied my apron. "Sam, two minutes?"

"Three," she said, which was her way of saying five .

We slipped through the back door into fog-wet air. The alley ran like a narrow river between brick—our café on one side, the museum's service wall on the other, everything beaded with moisture. Police tape hung at the museum's end, bright and brittle. A portable flood lamp glowed beyond, washing the side door in an anemic daylight.

We stayed on our side of sanity.

"Angle matters," Liam murmured, slipping his phone from his pocket. "If we shoot from here, we can zoom without crossing the line."

I crouched, eye level with the rippled asphalt. The city had resurfaced the alley two years ago and done it badly, which I now found myself grateful for. Cheap asphalt records stories like a notebook.

"There," I said. "See the dust? It's thin, but the pattern breaks where someone stepped."

He knelt, careful hands braced on his knees, and took shots in a slow clockwork—left, center, right. "Size maybe nine? Could be a woman or a man with small feet. Treads look generic."

"Generic is safe for criminals," I said. "How considerate of them."

Closer to our dumpster, a small black shard lay half-hidden in grit. I pointed, but didn't reach. "Is that—"

"Camera hinge," Liam finished. "From a bullet camera or a cheap dome cap. Could be ours, could be theirs."

I looked up at our exterior camera. Its bracket sat intact, smug as a gargoyle. "Not ours."

He angled his phone, capturing the shard by our dumpster with the museum door blurred beyond. The composition felt like an accident and a confession.

"Someone disabled a lens to get a clean path," he said, straightening. "Or dropped that after they did."

"We need to give this—the photos, the wristband—to Rangel," I said. "Soon."

"Agreed." Liam tucked his phone away. "Can we go inside first? My courage has a limited battery."

We stepped back into the café, bringing the alley's damp chill with us. Sam glanced up from the register, eyes on our hands. "Empty," I said quickly. "Just pictures."

"Good," she said. "Because the detective is back."

Officer Rangel stood at the end of the counter, hat in hand, clean lines etched into a face that had seen too much of last night.

"Morning again," he said. "Or what passes for one."

"Americano?" I asked, already reaching for a cup.

"Bless you," he said. "And... if you have a minute in the back?"

We passed through the swinging door into the prep area. The espresso machine's soft hum followed like an anxious cat.

"I'm aware you were near the alley earlier," Rangel began. "Don't worry—you didn't cross the tape. If you had, I'd be writing a different kind of report."

I nodded, relieved. "We stayed on our side. But we did find..." I slid the sandwich bag onto the stainless counter. "A staff wristband. In the cracks by our dumpster. It smells like—well, like the river. And we photographed what looks like footprints. And a broken camera hinge."

He studied the bag without touching it. His expression did something complicated. "Staff gray. That narrows some things."

"Were the staff supposed to exit through that door?" I asked, keeping my tone neutral.

"Not last night," he said. "And not through your alley. That's locked to the public, typically. We'll take this, if you don't mind."

"Please," I said. "I didn't want to keep it; I wanted to do the right thing without, you know, obstructing justice or becoming it."

A corner of his mouth quirked. "You'd be surprised how many people pick up evidence like seashells. Thank you for not being seashell people."

He slid the bag into a proper evidence envelope, labeled, dated, initialed. The sight steadied me. Procedures were boats in rough water.

"Two questions," he said, pen poised. "You catered last night; you left at what time?"

"Eleven-thirty," I said. "We stacked trays, checked with the director, and hauled our bins out the front."

"Any tension? Arguments?"

"Not that I saw. The director looked frazzled. Security Chief Pike looked tired but solid. The curator—Dr. Fred Barlow—kept vanishing and reappearing, like he had twelve hands and all of them were busy."

"Okay. Second question: Between midnight and one, did you hear anything from your loft?"

I took a breath. "A siren, brief. I saw blue light reflect on my ceiling. I figured it was a patrol car passing on Main."

"It wasn't," Rangel said. "It was ours. The museum's secondary sensor tripped and sent a silent callout. The lobby alarm never sounded."

Mabel had said it hadn't. The town had argued it had. Pike had died and the medallion had vanished. Barlow had disappeared.

And the lobby alarm never sounded.

"Is Dr. Barlow okay?" I asked, then amended, "Do you think he—"

"We don't know," Rangel said gently. "If you remember anything else—smells, sounds, shadows—call me. And let us do the investigating, yes?"
"Yes," I said, with all the sincerity I could brew.
He hesitated, then added, "Off the record—keep an eye on your back door. The square is going to get loud."
He left with his Americano and our hypothetical wristband, which felt less hypothetical by the second.
Sam re-buttoned her cardigan correctly and exhaled. "Okay. It's official: We are not picking up anything else. We are not crawling under anything. We are not—"
"Hattie," Liam interrupted, voice bright with polite desperation, "maybe you could call the museum and ask if they want a delivery of condolence pastries? That would be a legitimate reason to get inside, and I could, uh, drop off a… sympathy card? Near the Index Room?"
Sam looked between us like she was watching toddlers plan to climb a bookshelf. "Index Room?"
I showed her Mrs. Pickles's charred program with IR–28 scrawled along the bottom. "Archival code, I think. If we can get eyes on cubby twenty-eight—"
"No," Sam said.
"Just to check if a file is mis-shelved," I said.
"Still no."
"I'll go," Liam offered, because he has a heart made of both gold and poor risk assessment. "I look forgettable in a good way. I can carry a pastry box and ask for directions. If they say no, I will leave immediately. I will not touch anything. I will not become anything."
"Absolutely not," Sam said to both of us, then pinched her nose and groaned. "Fine. Fine. If you're going to do something questionably wise, at least do it legally. Deliver free muffins. Ask for the director to sign a receipt. If someone invites you down a hallway, so be it. But if you get arrested, I'm not wasting a good lawyer on you. I'll send Mabel."
Mabel, who had been hovering like a decorative gargoyle, popped her head around the corner. "I make a delightful character witness."
"See?" Sam said. "Terrifying."
We packed a condolence box—blueberry scones, almond croissants, two cinnamon knots—and a neat receipt for a zero-dollar invoice. Liam wrote "with sympathy" on a card, his letters careful, childish. He slid the card into an envelope, then promptly addressed it upside down. I replaced the envelope and patted his knuckles.
"Ready?" I asked.

"No," he said, which was another way of saying yes.

We crossed the square together. The fog had almost burned off, leaving sharp sun that made the tape look indecently bright. At the museum steps, a police volunteer manned a table and took down names. I smiled, offered the box, and asked for the director.

"Five minutes," the volunteer said, sympathy and suspicion in equal measure. "Stay in the lobby."

Inside, the air was cold and too clean. The medallion's display pedestal stood like an empty throne. I tried not to look at the corridor where a sheet had been wheeled past.

The museum director, a brisk woman with a bun so tight it could hold a grudge, appeared, took the box, and softened by about three degrees.

"Thank you," she said. "That's very kind."

"I'm so sorry," I said, and meant it. "We can deliver to the break room if that's easier."

She hesitated, then handed the box to a flustered clerk. "Ethan, take this back. And bring me the guest sign-in."

"Of course," Ethan said, clutching the pastries. He hurried down the side hall. Liam's gaze followed, polite as a shadow.

The director shifted papers on a clipboard, her thoughts clearly elsewhere. "If the police ask you for statements, please cooperate. We'll get through this."

"What about Dr. Barlow?" I asked softly. "Any word?"

Her mouth flattened. "He'll turn up."

"That sounds like a prayer," I said.

"That sounds like Maplewood," she countered, and with a thank you that was half-dismissal, returned to the officers conferring near the map of the Grant Wing.

Ethan came back with the volunteer and guest sheet but no pastries. The director's pen scratched signatures. Liam kept his eyes on his shoes.

We left without incident. My adrenaline, which had been living in my throat, settled to my shaking knees.

"The side hall," Liam murmured. "That's the way to the Index Room. I saw the sign in the corner by the water fountain."

I swallowed. "We'll try again. With an appointment. And a better excuse."

"Better than free pastries?" he said. "Impossible."

Back at the café, Mabel was waiting with both elbows on a table and three fresh rumors. Mrs. Pickles was perched by the window consulting the "Triumvirate" via speakerphone and telling them to project calm; the cats were reportedly unimpressed.

"Tell me something solid," Sam said, sliding into a chair. "Not rumors. Facts."

"Fact," I said. "Lobby alarm never sounded. Secondary sensor did. Fact: staff wristband in our alley, river mud on it. Fact: broken camera hinge by our dumpster. Fact: Director brisk, Barlow missing, Pike dead. Fact: IR–28 could be Index Room cubby twenty-eight."

"Fact," Liam added shyly. "I saw a sign for Index services down that side hall."

"Fact," Mabel said, raising a finger with theatrical gravitas. "Greg Benson already printed flyers for a 'support local business' event at his shop."

"Of course he did," I muttered.

Sam rubbed her temples. "And the police?"

"Grateful for the wristband," I said. "Mildly alarmed by our curiosity. Warned us to keep our door locked."

"Do that," she said. "And put the alley camera feed on loop. I don't care if the whole square is on national news. We'll still do lunch."

Liam perked up. "Camera feed I can handle."

He hooked his laptop to the little monitor by the back door. The alley appeared in foggy grayscale—our dumpster, the crumbled asphalt, a corner of police tape fluttering like a nervous thought. Watching it made my heart beat in my ears.

"IR–28," I whispered, tapping my notepad. "Index Room. Twenty-eight. It's not nothing, right?"

"Right," Liam said. "And if it is nothing, it'll lead to something."

"That is the kind of logic that gets people buried," Sam muttered.

"Only during business hours," I promised.

Beans chose that moment to saunter in from the loft stairs and leap onto the prep counter with the grace of a gymnast and the entitlement of a monarch. He stretched, yawned, and dropped a second scrap of paper from somewhere on his person like a magician with an extra scarf.

I picked it up. Museum brochure. A corner torn off, showing a faint gray rectangle where a room label had been.

Liam tilted his head. "Storage."

"Storage where?"

He shrugged. "That's the trick."

For a long minute, none of us spoke. The café hummed, the square buzzed, the world tilted toward noon. Somewhere across that stretch of brick and glass, Owen Pike had died. Somewhere, Fred Barlow was a question mark. Somewhere, a medallion was either hidden or gone, and a list of transactions with too many zeros sat waiting in a drawer.

"You're going to keep going," Sam said, resigned.

"Yes," I said.

"Then do it right," she said. "Lists. Rules. Witnesses. Do not—under any circumstances—get yourself arrested or dead."

Mabel raised her latte. "To rules, then."

Mrs. Pickles raised her phone. "The Triumvirate approves."

Liam raised nothing, just looked at me with that anxious, brave expression and said, "I'll bring my notebook."

I looked at the alley feed—empty, innocuous, a river of concrete biding its time—and felt the knot in my shoulders turn into a line, an arrow pointing forward.

"Motive. Means. Mud," I said.

"And muffins," Sam added.

"Yes," I said, smiling despite myself. "We'll need those too."

The Index Code

The police had thinned by lunchtime, but the air still tasted like tension. It hung in the square, clinging to lampposts and gossip. The yellow tape around the museum looked like a badly wrapped gift no one wanted to open.
I poured another round of lattes, but my mind wasn't in the foam. It was fixed on the penciled letters from Mrs. Pickles's charred program: IR–28.
It wasn't just a scribble, I felt like it had to mean something. Mrs. Pickles didn't believe in coincidences, and honestly, neither did I.
Liam was hunched over his laptop at the corner table, a cinnamon knot in one hand, scrolling through the museum's public site with the other.
"Nothing on 'IR–28,'" he said. "No exhibit by that code, no artifact tag, no event room labeled that way. I even checked the museum's archives index—what little of it's online."
"Archives?" I asked, sliding him a refill. "As in… Index Room?"
He looked up. "How did you—"
"I was reading the museum brochure while pretending to clean," I said. "There's an Index Room listed in the staff map, but it's for cataloging donations. If the gala program said IR–28, maybe it's referring to a file or shelf."
Liam's brows lifted. "Hattie, that's… actually possible. Those codes look like archival designations."
"Then we have our first breadcrumb."
Sam approached, towel slung over one shoulder. "If you two are planning another field trip, tell me now so I can prewrite the apology email to the police."
"We're not planning anything," I said, which wasn't technically untrue. "We're exploring… curiosity."
Sam sighed. "That's what you said before we accidentally uncovered a counterfeit art scandal in fifth grade."
"That was a school project," I said.
"And this is a crime scene," she countered.
Liam closed his laptop. "Maybe I could visit legitimately," he said. "Ask if they need tech help recovering their backups. The police probably copied the servers, but local systems—"
Sam raised a hand. "No hacking."
"It's not hacking if I'm invited," Liam said, grinning. "It's polite curiosity with a keyboard."

By two, the lunch rush had faded. I packed a small box of pastries—our "condolence special"—and wrote a note in my neatest handwriting: For the staff of the Maplewood Museum. Thinking of you.

It wasn't deceit if kindness was involved.

Liam volunteered to carry the box. "If they let me past the lobby, I'll look for an Index Room sign. Just a peek."

I handed him the receipt clipboard. "You're taking this too. Deliveries need paperwork. Bureaucracy opens doors."

As he left, Mrs. Pickles swept in, draped in chiffon and mystery. She beamed at me. "I dreamed of corridors last night."

"That sounds claustrophobic," I said.

"There were whispers about numbers. Twos and eights," she went on. "One of my colleagues—Sir Whiskers—woke me at precisely two twenty-eight. That's a sign."

"Of insomnia," I muttered, but she was already twirling toward the pastry case, humming an ominous tune.

I didn't believe in her dreams, but I did believe in timing. And two twenty-eight was starting to feel prophetic.

Liam returned an hour later, slightly out of breath and smelling faintly of floor polish.

"Well?" I asked.

"I found it," he said, setting down the clipboard. "Index Room, ground floor, west corridor. Small, fluorescent, lined with cubbies labeled IR–1 through IR–50. I didn't go inside; a clerk was there. But you'll never guess what was on the open shelf near the door."

"What?"

He grinned, nervous energy sparking behind his eyes. "A box labeled IR–28. Half empty. Someone had pulled files recently."

My pulse quickened. "You're sure?"

"I'm sure enough to risk mild dehydration," he said. "It looked like financial documents—stamped forms, legal-sized paper, something about land usage."

Land usage. My mind leapt to the copies I'd already seen with Grant Developers' name on them.

Before I could reply, Mabel Cho entered, waving her phone like a flag. "Have you seen this?" she asked, thrusting the screen under my nose. "Breaking news—Councilwoman Grant's committee approved an emergency redevelopment motion this morning. It's already moving to vote."

Sam froze mid-swipe with her cloth. "Redevelopment of what?"

Mabel tapped the headline. "'Heritage Restoration Corridor.' That's the museum's street, plus three surrounding properties. Half the square."

I met Liam's eyes. "The museum's land."

"Which they can't sell," he said slowly, "unless they prove the current assets are compromised. Like, say, an unsolved theft and a dead security chief."

The café felt colder.

Mabel leaned in, conspiratorial. "Rumor says Grant's company is buying through a third-party shell. But you didn't hear it from me."

"Of course not," I said.

She smiled brightly. "So, what's new with you?"

"Same old," I said. "Coffee, crime, corruption."

She beamed. "Small towns are never boring."

By four, the square had settled into gray calm. The museum looked smaller under the overcast sky, less like a landmark and more like a wounded animal wrapped in plastic barriers. I found myself pacing between the espresso machine and the front windows, mind replaying every detail.

Index room, Land records. Councilwoman Grant. Pike's death. Missing curator.

And river mud.

Why river mud?

I grabbed my notepad and drew three columns: Who, What, Why. My handwriting turned cramped and urgent.

- Who: Pike, Barlow, Grant, maybe someone else.
- What: Medallion stolen, land papers missing, staff wristband in alley.
- Why: Redevelopment motive? Cover-up? Obviously something to hide?

Beans walked by, tail flicking across my notes.

"You have thoughts?" I asked.

He meowed once, definitive.

"Brilliant," I said. "We'll add that to the list."

Liam returned from the back, laptop open. "I might've found something else. The museum's Wi-Fi logs are public-facing; they publish data for visitors to monitor outages. Between 11:50 and 12:10 last night, there was a full blackout."

"During the gala cleanup," I said. "When we were packing trays."

"Exactly," he said. "Someone cut power to internal routers. Could be normal maintenance—but that's the same window the medallion vanished and Pike apparently died."

The pieces were starting to assemble themselves into a shape I didn't like.

A knock at the front door interrupted. Officer Rangel stood there again, weary but sharp-eyed. I let him in.

He gestured toward an empty table. "Mind if we sit?"

"Of course," I said, motioning him to the corner booth.

He set down a file folder. "I wanted to thank you for the wristband and your cooperation. Forensics confirms it belonged to museum staff. Mud traces match the river embankment south of here."

"So someone did come from the river," I said. "But why?"

"Could've used the tunnel," he said, watching my reaction.

"What tunnel?"

He smiled faintly. "Ah. You don't know. There's an old service tunnel under the museum, sealed decades ago. Rumor says it connects to the warehouse near the river."

Liam and I exchanged glances.

"Don't get ideas," Rangel warned. "We're sealing both ends tomorrow."

He rose, thanked me for the coffee, and left before I could ask more.

The second the door shut, Liam whispered, "Tunnel."

"I heard," I said.

"River mud."

"I heard that too."

We stared at each other, then at Beans, who blinked once, slow and judgmental.

"Well," I said, "we've officially gone from curious bystanders to possibly the only people paying attention."

"Is that safe?" Liam asked.

"No," I said. "But it's interesting."

After closing, I climbed to my loft with the day still buzzing under my skin. I brewed one last cup for myself, sat by the window, and looked down at the dark square. Police lights flickered faintly near the museum, now half-silhouetted by fog. Beyond the cordon, the side door where the staff wristband had been looked ordinary again.

Too ordinary.

I set my mug down and opened my notepad to a fresh page.

Questions:

- If the index room holds land records, why hide them?
- What does Grant gain from Pike's death?
- Where's Dr. Barlow?
- Why is the tunnel sealed?

Beans hopped onto the sill and pressed his paw against the glass, eyes fixed on something outside. I followed his gaze.

A single figure crossed the square, coat collar up, moving fast along the museum wall before vanishing into the alley. My pulse quickened. Too dark to tell who—but the shape was lean, deliberate.

"Liam's going to hate this," I murmured, reaching for my phone.

Outside, the square returned to stillness, but the calm didn't fool me. Maplewood wasn't quiet. It was holding its breath.

And I had a feeling the next exhale would change everything.

Councilwoman on Camera

Soon , Maplewood had dressed itself for damage control.
Across the square, the museum's steps were swept clean of tape, as if an overnight miracle could erase a crime scene. A podium appeared beneath the marble columns, flanked by flags and ferns, and a banner fluttered above it reading Heritage Strong. A small crowd gathered, drawn by rumor and civic curiosity. From my café window, it looked less like mourning and more like a photo opportunity.
Sam appeared beside me with her coffee. "Guess who's hosting the show?"
"I'll give you one guess and a string of pearls," I said.
Right on cue, Councilwoman Dolores Grant ascended the steps. Press microphones glinted under the gray light as she spread her hands in a well-rehearsed display of compassion.
Liam stood behind the counter, fiddling with a coil of wires. "I brought a better mount for the alley camera," he said, shyly. "Our current one faces the dumpster. I can adjust it to catch the walkway without breaking any privacy laws."
Sam sighed. "Since when do we need surveillance for muffins?"
"Since someone left us keys and corpses," I said. "Do it."
He smiled faintly and disappeared into the back with his toolkit. Through the window, Grant's amplified voice rolled across the square.
"Maplewood is united in grief," she said, every syllable polished. "We will honor Owen Pike and continue our mission to preserve our town's cultural legacy."
Polite applause followed, hesitant as the weather. I watched her face, waiting for something unscripted—a tic, a slip, a truth that didn't fit the stage. There it was: a small, nervous brush across her wrist before she clasped her hands again. A tiny fracture in a porcelain smile.
Sam leaned close. "You see that?"
"I see everything," I said.
The mayor stepped up next, pledging transparency, restoration, and additional security. Mabel Cho, who had found the perfect seat outside my window, texted someone furiously while balancing her muffin. Mrs. Pickles hovered behind her, draped in velvet and mystery, mouthing words I couldn't hear.
I had a feeling the cats had briefed her.

By ten o'clock, the speech ended. The councilwoman waved to cameras, shook the mayor's hand, and retreated toward the museum's side door. Liam emerged from the back, wiping dust from his fingers.
"Camera's up," he said. "Wide angle on the alley and the square corner. We'll catch anyone cutting through."
"Good," I said. "Now we wait."
Mabel burst in moments later, newspaper in hand. "Did you hear the latest? Grant's already proposing a redevelopment fund to 'strengthen local heritage infrastructure.' You know what that means?"
"Bureaucratic nonsense?" I offered.
"Condos," she said darkly. "Overpriced condos with French balconies that overlook the crime scene."
"Lovely view," Sam muttered.
Mabel leaned across the counter. "Mark my words—she's behind this. Power goes missing the same time she's pushing her project? It's Maplewood math."
"She could just be opportunistic," I said.
"Or both," she said, sipping foam off her latte. "Opportunistic people make great villains."
"Stop giving my life foreshadowing," I said.

After lunchtime, business slowed enough for me to check the alley monitor. The new camera feed displayed a clean view of the passage—our door, the bins, the museum wall. All empty, all ordinary. Which was somehow worse.
"Liam," I called. "Pull yesterday's feed again. The night before the gala."
He joined me, clicking through clips on his laptop. Hours sped by in jump cuts—trash trucks, delivery vans, passing cats. Then one frame froze my attention.
Two figures moved through the edge of the alley, heads down, carrying boxes. The timestamp: 9:42 p.m., two nights before the gala.
"Zoom," I said.
He did. The grain turned ugly, but the outline was unmistakable. Councilwoman Grant in a long coat, walking beside a man in a dark blazer. Trent. Her consultant.
They weren't sneaking exactly, but they weren't strolling either.
"They're using the alley," Liam said. "From the museum toward Main. What's back there?"
"Nothing," I said. "Just service doors. Storage."

He scrubbed the timeline forward. At 9:44, they vanished into the dark. Two minutes later, a flicker of light appeared briefly under the museum's side door—like a flashlight being turned off.
Sam joined us, drying her hands. "What are we looking at?"
"Potential blackmail material," I said. "Or a really awkward date."

At two, the bell chimed and Officer Rangel stepped inside. He ordered a coffee, thanked us for yesterday's cooperation, and then quietly said, "Do you have a minute?"
We went into the back room, where the refrigerator hummed creating cover for any conversation not intended to be overheard.

"I'm sure you've been looking at your security feed again," he said. His tone wasn't accusatory, just tired and almost as if speaking to himself.

"We look at it daily," I said. "Health code requires it."
He gave me a look that said he'd been on the force too long to buy that. "Anything unusual?"
I hesitated, then pulled up the 9:42 clip. "Unusual enough."
He watched in silence. The muscle in his jaw flexed once. "Can I get a copy?," he said finally. "And after that, don't talk about it. Don't show anyone.
Understand?"
I nodded. "Is she a suspect?"
"She's a politician," he said. "That's a long way of saying: yes and no."
He pocketed the flash drive, thanked me for the coffee, and left.
I didn't bring up the fact that his coffee wasn't a courtesy coffee, but he'd left.

When I returned to the counter, Sam raised an eyebrow. "Was that your 'don't worry' face or your 'I'm worried' face?"
"The latter," I said. "And it's getting worse."

We closed a bit early, due to slow business. Really, I just wanted quiet. Maplewood after sunset felt too peaceful, too poised. I checked the alley again through the monitor. Mist curled along the bricks, catching the orange glow of the streetlights.
At 9:11, two teenagers zipped past with skateboards. At 9:20, a trash truck rumbled through. At 9:37, nothing. Then—movement.

A figure in a dark coat appeared on the museum side, carrying a long case—something like a rolled poster or a drafting tube. They moved quickly, hugging the wall. Another figure followed a few seconds later, smaller, scanning the path behind them like a lookout.

Liam leaned close to the screen. "Not Grant. Not Trent either."

The first disappeared toward the square; the second paused, turned their head, and looked straight at our camera. For a split second, I saw the outline of a hat, the glint of eyes that knew exactly where the lens was. Then they pulled the brim lower and walked away.

The monitor went still.

A minute later, a soft clink at the front door made me flinch. Something metallic slid under the glass and clattered across the floor, coming to rest by Beans's paw.

A key.

I locked the door then picked it up. A small tag dangled from it, cracked and yellow: West Maintenance.

Liam whispered, "That's the museum's rear wing."

I met his eyes. "Someone wants us to find something."

"Or to walk into a trap," Sam said grimly.

"Could be both."

We sealed the key in a plastic bag and placed it under the counter. The café lights cast long shadows across the floor. Beans stretched, yawned, and thumped his tail, unimpressed with human drama.

"Tomorrow," I said quietly. "We tell Rangel everything. Tonight, we keep the doors locked."

Liam nodded. "And we back up the footage twice."

"Make it three times," Sam said. "I'm starting to believe redundancy is our only superpower."

Outside, Maplewood glimmered soft and safe again. Inside, it wasn't. Not really.

Because now we had a key to something that should've stayed locked— and a camera that someone already knew existed.

The Curator Vanishes

By dawn, the square had gone from stage-managed grief to practical cleanup. The ferns were gone; the podium was stacked behind the museum hedges like a folded promise. Fog dragged its feet along Main, and the air held that thin, metallic chill that makes coffee smell braver. I was halfway down the stairs from my loft when my phone buzzed. A text from an unknown number: "Keep your door locked." No signature. No context.

"Good morning to you too," I told the banister and kept moving.

Sam was already in the café, sleeves rolled to her elbows, counting the till with the competent fury of a woman who can out-organize a tornado. Liam came in moments later with a pastry box and a look that suggested he'd slept approximately nine minutes.

He set the box on the counter. "Almond croissants. For morale."

"Bless you," I said, then showed them the text.

Sam's mouth pinched. "Rangel?"

"Number's blocked."

"So… a friend," Liam said, and then, because he has a soft heart and a sturdy fear of reality, added, "or a friend who doesn't know how to be a friend."

"Either way," I said, "we're keeping it locked."

We did the opening dance with a little more choreography—lights, grinders, ovens. The alley camera feed purred along on the back-room monitor, a gray ribbon that watched while we brewed. At six-thirty, I dialed Rangel and left a message about the key: West Maintenance. "We didn't touch the lock," I added. "We won't."

By seven, the first wave of regulars had arrived: teachers, nurses, a dog walker whose clients were more famous than some council members. Maplewood needed caffeine and comfort, and Brewed Awakening supplied both in to-go cups.

Mabel Cho swooped to the counter in a scarf that could double as a flag. "News!" she announced, then leaned in as if we had a classified clearance. "The museum sent a bulletin to staff at six a.m. Dr. Barlow is officially listed as missing, not merely 'unavailable for comment.' They've asked for tips and prayers."

Something in my chest tightened. "Prayers don't substitute for searches."

"Don't let the council hear you say that," she said, then lowered her voice. "Also, rumor has it Grant's been at City Hall since five. Either she's spinning or she's sweating."

"Or both," I said.

Mrs. Vera Pickles glided in next, velvet and perfume and the clink of bracelets. She placed a neat paper-wrapped parcel on the counter with the ceremony of a coronation. "For you," she said.

"Please tell me that's not a séance kit," I said.

"Don't be gauche, dear. It's evidence."

Inside the paper: a short pencil stub with Maplewood Museum stamped in tiny gold letters. The eraser was flattened, graphite blunted down to a wedge.

"Found on my balcony," she said, pleased with her cats' continued competence. "Sir Whiskers pushed it under the curtains."

"Your cats have better sourcing than some newspapers," I said.

"Obviously," she said. "They also prefer chicken pate over ocean whitefish, in case it comes up."

I bagged the pencil and wrote the time on the label. The act steadied me. We handed out croissants and kindness until the line curled out the door, people holding paper cups like talismans against a world that kept not being polite.

At eight-fifteen, Officer Rangel walked in, hat pulled low, face sharper with lack of sleep. He took the key from the evidence bag, turned it over once, and let out a breath that told me it meant something.

"We've been looking for this," he said. "West Maintenance opens the corridor behind the grant wing—equipment rooms, service closet, access to the old vault door. Don't worry," he added, catching my expression. "You're not the only people who got a mysterious delivery last night. The assistant director had a manila envelope shoved under her door. Blank. No prints."

"Someone using courier tactics without the courage to knock," I said.

He nodded. "We'll treat this properly. Thank you."

"Detective," Sam said—too formal for our town, which is why she got his attention. "Dr. Barlow?"

He hesitated just long enough to make me hate him for it. "We don't have him," he said. "Yet. If he's hiding, he's good at it. If he's not—" He didn't finish.

He left with black coffee and a promise to call if the key led somewhere immediate. The café door swung shut behind him, and silence expanded into the space he'd occupied like a rubber band snapping back.

Liam exhaled into his hands. "Okay," he said, falsely bright. "Today's plan?"

"Work," Sam said. "You two are going to work."

"Also," I said, "we're going to the museum at noon with a tray of free sandwiches, because grief eats, and we are generous."
Sam stared at me for a beat, then conceded with a sigh. "Fine. But the tray goes no farther than the lobby."
"Of course," I said. "Lobbies are where all the best eavesdropping happens."
She rolled her eyes. "If you get arrested for eavesdropping, I'm putting it on a T-shirt."

At noon, Maplewood's gray lifted into a pale, apologetic sun. Liam and I crossed the square with a tray of turkey and brie on house-made baguette, a stack of napkins, and a note that read With sympathy, Brewed Awakening. The police volunteer at the table recognized us from yesterday and, after a quick glance at our bag, waved us into the foyer. The museum felt wrong without its ambient chatter and docent smiles. The medallion's pedestal stood like an empty throne; the marble echoed with soft footsteps and a duct's low hum. The director—bun stern, blouse immaculate—materialized like a warning label.
"You again," she said, though her tone had gratitude baked in. "You brought… sandwiches."
"Sometimes grief eats," I said. "And we had extra."
She hesitated, then guided us to a side table. "Break room's overflowing," she said. "Between the police and the press… we're a nest of hornets."
"I'm so sorry," I said, and meant it. "Any word on Dr. Barlow?"
Her mouth compressed. "He knows how to disappear when donors demand too much," she said. "He does not know how to disappear from this."
"He's probably scared," I said softly.
"He's probably proud," she countered. "Which is another kind of fear."
She took a sandwich, managed half a smile, and went to scold a cameraman who had wandered into a rope line.

A young clerk—Ethan, judging by the bottlecap badge—sidled up for some of the delivery food. "Thanks," he said. "It's been… crazy here."
"I can imagine." I pitched my voice an inch more casual. "Index Room's probably getting a workout?"
He blinked, startled. "Im not following? "

"Everyone in town did a shift here at some point in high school." I said. "I loved the catalog system. All those little labeled cubbies. IR–28 had a good squeak when you pulled it."

He snorted a laugh. "It still does," he said. Then flinched as if he was too casual. "I mean—uh—procedures—" He then stuffed his pastry in his mouth too fast and escaped down the hall.

Liam and I exchanged a look.
"IR–28 is still squeaky," I murmured.

"Love when clues confirm with a squeak," he said, deadpan.
We lingered in the lobby longer than necessary and learned very little on purpose and a few things by accident: a security camera near the west corridor had been "out for maintenance"; a box of HDMI cables had gone missing; someone had ordered too many granola bars in a panic and now the entire staff was cranky with oats.
On the way out, I paused at a display case near the museum shop. Condensation had fogged the inside of the glass at the lower edge, as if someone had touched the seam with a warm hand. Not a crime. Not nothing.
Outside, the square looked harmless again. Greg Benson stood in Bean Temple's doorway holding a to-go cup and an expression that said even my coffee is smug. He lifted the cup in a toast. "How's the grief-catering business?"
"Crowded," I said.
"Tell your customers we're donating ten percent of today's proceeds to 'Heritage Security,'" he said, making air quotes I wanted to confiscate.
"We believe in safety."
"We believe in facts," I said.
"That too," he said, and sipped as if victory had a flavor.
Mabel intercepting us on the sidewalk was a mercy. "The council just posted their agenda," she said, breathless with glee. "Emergency session tonight. Heritage Corridor, item one."
"Transparency at the speed of bulldozers," I said.
She slipped a half-sheet from her tote. "Also, rumor says there's a private buyer circling for the warehouse by the river. If the city sells—"
"The tunnel gets a new landlord," Liam finished.
We exchanged a look that was equal parts dread and calculation.

"Don't do anything rash," Mabel said, which, coming from Mabel, meant call me when you do.

Back at the café, the afternoon dripped by with the slow drama of a leaky faucet. The alley monitor showed ordinary things doing ordinary jobs—delivery vans, a pair of pigeons arguing with conviction, a child dragging a stick along the brick for the percussive joy of it.

At three, a figure hovered at our door and then disappeared when I looked up. At three-oh-five, the phone rang and no one spoke. At three-ten, Mrs. Pickles returned to order a tea and to inform me that her cats had, and I quote, "expressed deep concern about municipal embezzlement."

"Did they suggest a remedy?" I asked.

"Sardines," she said. "But that's their remedy for everything."

At four-thirty, Liam and I sat with our notebooks and turned our puzzle into a list that felt like a rope we could climb:

- Key (West Maintenance) → Now with Rangel. Corridor to grant wing equipment rooms.
- IR–28 → Active, half-empty. Clerk flinched. Land records likely inside.
- Grant + Trent (9:42 p.m., two nights pre-gala) → Boxes through alley. Unofficial presence.
- Tunnel to River → Rumor confirmed by Rangel; warehouse buyer rumored.
- Lobby alarm → Never sounded; secondary sensor triggered around midnight.
- Pike → Gift shop receipt 11:57 p.m. (cash, initials O.P.) alive before midnight.
- Barlow → Officially missing. Hiding or hidden.

Sam set down three cappuccinos with the air of a medic delivering morphine. "Add this," she said, tapping our list. "Rule: nothing alone. If you're going somewhere weird, you text me first and you go with someone who can drag you out by your apron."

"Define weird," I said.

"Anything with a plaque," she said. "Or a lock."

"Noted."

At five, the square tilted toward evening. Streetlights blinked alive like cautious stars. A breeze lifted the edges of our chalkboard sign and flipped it up so it read TODAY'S SPECIAL: STAY ALIVE. I left it. Felt accurate.

The alley feed, so far a study in boredom, hiccuped. Static fuzzed across the image for three seconds, then cleared. When it did, a shape hovered just at the edge of the museum wall—small, hunched, unsure. The assistant. She looked over her shoulder twice, then, in a blur of motion, darted to our back door and rapped a staccato rhythm: three taps, pause, two taps.

I was already moving when Sam hissed, "Hattie—"

"Witnesses," I said, and waved them to follow.

I opened the door on the chain and saw a face I'd only glimpsed in corridors: museum assistant—mid-twenties, eyes too wide, hands too cold.

"Help me," she whispered. "Please."

"Inside," I said, and unlocked the chain.

She slipped in, a shiver in human form. Liam shut the door; Sam threw the bolt. The assistant pressed her back to the wall as if she needed something solid to stop the shaking.

"I didn't kill him," she said without prompting, which is one of those sentences that guarantees you won't finish your coffee. "Pike confronted Trent in the west hall. They argued about the drives. I heard it. I ran."

"Drives?" I asked. My voice was steady, because baristas learn to sound steady even when the world tilts.

"Hard drives," she said. "The ones with land records. Trent was moving them. Pike said it was a crime. Grant—" She stopped like the word had cut her. "She told us to keep our heads down, that the grant wing needed refurbishing and 'what donors don't know won't hurt them.'"

"Where's Dr. Barlow?" I asked.

Her eyes filled. "Hiding," she said. "Or he was. He said he had proof and then he stopped answering."

"Where proof?" Liam asked gently.

She swallowed. "Index Room. IR–28. And the clock tower. He liked heights." She fumbled in her coat and produced something that looked like it had burned her to hold—a museum maintenance card on a lanyard, cracked, scuffed, stamped with TEMP ACCESS . And a small brass key tied with dental floss. "If you hand these over, I'm dead. If you use them, you might not be."

"Those aren't choices," Sam said, and I loved her fiercely for saying it.

The assistant wiped her nose with the heel of her hand. "Grant called an emergency session for the corridor," she said. "If the vote passes, they can seal rooms, relocate collections, 'reallocate' assets. The drives could vanish legally. You have to—" She stopped, panic spiking behind her eyes. "I shouldn't be here."

A shadow crossed the alley camera—a shape passing the door—and the assistant flattened into the wall again. We all froze. The shape kept going. The monitor returned to empty gray.

I found my voice. "We'll get you to Rangel," I said. "Safely. Tonight."

She shook her head. "They watch the station. They watch everything."

"Then we call him here," Sam said, thumb already on her phone.

"Blocked numbers," I said. "Use the landline."

Liam dialed. Rangel answered on the third ring, voice compressed by too many rooms with too many problems. I kept it simple: We have someone terrified you need to hear. Can you come to the back door in five without lights? He could. He would.

We hid the assistant in the prep alcove with a glass of water and a cinnamon knot, because we are local and comfort is our weapon. When Rangel knocked—a soft, specific rhythm—we opened to let him in. He didn't bring another officer. He brought a notebook and a face that had room for one more bad thing.

The assistant spoke in small, cracked sentences; he wrote them down in neat, slanted script. When she faltered, Sam refilled her water and said nothing. When she cried, Beans appeared, and pressed his warm, indifferent body against her calf until her breath remembered how to be useful.

Rangel took the lanyard and the key with hands that treated them like small explosives. "You understand these go into evidence," he said gently. "You'll be protected."

She nodded like the word meant a different language. "Will you find him?" she asked—Barlow in the empty of her voice.

"We'll try," he said. He meant it.

We slid her out the front under a quilted coat, and Rangel guided her to an unmarked car like it was a life raft. The square had softened into evening. Grant's office lights burned warm rectangles into the council building across town. Somewhere, Mabel was writing three versions of this story with different adjectives.

When I returned inside, the smell of vanilla and coffee wrapped around me. Ordinary. Glorious. Fragile.

Liam set down his pen. "Clock tower," he said. "Index Room. IR–28. Drives."

"And the vote tonight," Sam added. "They'll try to move faster than the truth."

I looked at the alley feed. The path lay empty, the world more dangerous for what we now knew. I pressed a palm to the glass of the back door and felt the faint vibration of the city through it, as if Maplewood itself were humming in its sleep.

"Tomorrow," I said, "we do this by the book. Tonight, we lock our doors, back up our footage, and try to sleep."

"And the tower?" Liam asked.

"Daylight," I said. "Because I like my mysteries with witnesses."

Beans thumped his tail once. Approval. Or boredom. With him, it's a thin line.

We turned the sign to CLOSED and dimmed the lights. Outside, the museum's windows stared across the square like dark eyes. Somewhere between their sheen and the clock's slow hands, a curator had vanished, a security chief had died, and a town's past was being rearranged.

And somewhere, a very tidy councilwoman was running out of places to hide.

Bitter Evidence

The morning after the assistant showed up in our café, Maplewood behaved as if nothing had happened. That's the strange thing about small towns: tragedy doesn't stop the trash trucks or the morning joggers. It just adds another whisper to the air.
I woke to the sound of Beans scratching at my closet door—a reminder that breakfast waits for no one, not even the accidentally entangled. Downstairs, Sam already had the café lights glowing and the smell of fresh bread doing its best to argue that everything was fine. It wasn't.
She looked up when I entered. "You didn't sleep."
"Neither did you."
Liam arrived five minutes later with his laptop tucked under one arm, hair half-tamed, expression caught between determined and terrified.
"Rangel texted," he said, sliding into a booth. "He took the assistant to a safe location last night. She's under temporary protection."
"That's something," Sam said, pouring him coffee.
"He also confirmed the West Maintenance key fits an old steel door behind the Grant Wing. They've posted a guard, but he didn't say why." He hesitated. "I think he found something."
"Something," I echoed. "That's helpful."
Liam glanced at me. "He's on duty until noon. After that, we can ask."
Sam folded her arms. "Or we can run the café, like sensible humans."
"We can do both," I said. "Multitasking is part of my skill set."

By eight, Brewed Awakening was packed again. Word about the missing curator had spread; everyone had an opinion. Mabel Cho leaned on the counter, conspiratorial as always.
"People are saying the curator stole it himself," she whispered. "Ran off with the medallion, left poor Pike to clean up the mess."
"People say a lot of things," I said, tamping espresso. "Usually because they like stories more than truth."
She smiled slyly. "Isn't that what mystery writers say?"
"I just pour the coffee," I said.
Mrs. Pickles breezed in behind her, velvet sleeves trailing like fog.
"Nonsense," she declared. "Dr. Barlow wouldn't steal anything. His aura was far too academic for crime. However"—she leaned in—"the spirits have been restless. My cats took turns staring at the clock tower all night."
"Because the clock ticks," I said.

"Exactly," she said, delighted I'd agreed with her on anything.
Sam mouthed save me over Mrs. Pickles's shoulder. I mouthed back later.
Liam appeared from the back, holding his laptop like it was radioactive. "You should see this," he said, and we ducked behind the counter while Sam handled orders.
He pulled up our alley feed from just before dawn. The screen showed fog rolling past the dumpsters, a faint movement in the shadows near the museum's wall—then a flash, like a lighter flicking once.
"What is that?" I asked.
He rewound, slowed it down. The light reflected off something metallic near the lower wall, right above a maintenance vent.
"It's not a lighter," he said. "It's a reflection. From glass. Like a lens."
I leaned closer. "Someone installed another camera."
He nodded. "And not ours. See how it blinks? It's transmitting. That means someone else is watching the alley, probably remote."
"Rangel?" I asked.
"Maybe. Or someone pretending to be him."

We decided to walk the square at lunch under the excuse of "delivering flyers." Maplewood was bright with winter sun; everything looked too ordinary for secrets. Near the museum, yellow tape had been replaced by a polite sign: Closed for Restoration. A lie with good typography.
Officer Rangel spotted us from the steps and waved us over. "You two need quieter hobbies," he said, but his smile had gratitude baked in.
"Did you find anything behind the west door?" I asked.
He hesitated. "We found boxes," he said finally. "Old exhibit cases and some crates with museum markings. One was half-open. Inside were fragments of something—porcelain, maybe ceramic. Could be debris, could be broken art. Forensics is checking. But that's not the strange part."
"Define strange," Liam said.
"One of the crates had fresh tape labeled 'Donor Archives.' Inside— burned folders, still warm when we found them. Somebody tried to destroy records last night."
I felt a chill crawl up my arms. "Records from the Index Room?"
"Looks that way," he said. "Your friend Grant will have a lot of explaining to do."
"She's not my friend," I said.

He handed me a card. "If anything new shows up—anyone hovering, anything out of place—call. We've got more eyes on this than I can count."

When he left, Liam and I circled around the museum's east side, where a temporary fence kept curious citizens back. Through the gaps, I saw workers hauling bins, not in uniform, but moving with the precision of people who didn't want to be noticed. One looked up briefly—tan coat, baseball cap. Our camera had caught that silhouette before.

"Trent," I whispered.

Liam nodded, pulling out his phone and snapping a single photo. "If he's doing this in daylight, he's either bold or desperate."

"Maybe both," I said.

Back at the café, Sam was watching the local news on her tablet.

"Listen," she said, turning up the volume.

Councilwoman Grant stood on-screen, framed by City Hall's oak doors, reporters circling her like gnats. "The museum's board is cooperating fully with the ongoing investigation," she said smoothly. "I am confident we'll restore Maplewood's faith in its cultural institutions."

I frowned. "You hear that phrasing? Restore faith? That's what people say when they're already guilty."

"Or when they know they're next," Sam said.

"Where's the council vote?" I asked.

"Tonight," she said. "Six o'clock. Emergency session."

"Perfect timing," I said. "Right before evidence can catch up."

At five, the café emptied except for regulars who treated us like an extension of their living rooms. Liam checked the alley feed again, scrubbing through frames. The new mystery camera blinked steadily near the museum wall, pointing slightly downward toward the vent.

"That vent connects to the old sub-basement," he said. "The one sealed decades ago."

"The tunnel," I said.

He nodded. "If someone's still using it, that camera isn't for safety. It's a lookout."

"Then let's test it," I said.

He blinked. "How?"

I grabbed a flashlight from the drawer and a chalk stick from the specials board. "We walk the alley, mark where it sees us, then stay where it can't."

Sam glared. "No. Absolutely not. You're not crawling near vents while I'm still digesting dinner."

"Just looking," I promised. "From our side."

The alley was silvered with fog again. The new camera lens caught the streetlight and blinked faintly, a tiny, artificial star. Liam stood where it could see him; I moved sideways along the wall, watching its angle. When I reached a narrow alcove beside a drainpipe, the light disappeared. "Blind spot," I said.

He joined me, voice low. "If someone's using that vent, they can pass objects through it without being seen."

"Or someone already did," I said. "And we just found their window."

Something metallic clinked softly under my shoe. I bent and found a sliver of brass shaped like a key fragment—broken at the bow. Etched letters still visible: ...INT WING.

"The rest of the West Maintenance key," I said. "Someone snapped it off."

We sealed it in a bag before Sam could start yelling. Back inside, I labeled it with the time. Rangel would need it, but I needed to see what it fit first.

At six, the council meeting streamed live on the mayor's YouTube channel—modern transparency for a town allergic to it. Sam put it on the big screen for the few regulars lingering over scones. Grant presided at the table, flanked by bored colleagues. The motion read: Emergency approval for partial restoration of museum west facilities and transfer of property to city holding trust.

"Translation," Liam muttered, "legal control of the land until redevelopment."

"And once it's city property," I said, "records vanish into bureaucracy."

Grant smiled on screen, every inch the public servant. "We move forward with hope," she said. "For Maplewood's future."

The vote passed, five to two. The gavel fell. The chat feed exploded. The past, quite literally, had been sold.

I turned off the tablet. "We need proof she doctored those records."

"Or someone with access to her files," Liam said quietly. "The assistant said Barlow hid copies."

"Index Room and the clock tower," I said. "Tomorrow we start with daylight."

He nodded, already thinking. "If we can get into the tower—"

Sam cut him off. "You'll do it after coffee service, not before."

I laughed, but it came out tired. "Deal."

That night, the square fell silent by ten. Fog rolled thicker than before, muffling everything. The museum's windows glowed dimly from emergency lights, pale and hollow.

From my loft, I watched through the curtain as a single figure crossed the square—tall coat, steady stride, purposeful. Councilwoman Grant. She stopped beneath the clock tower, head tilted as if listening to something inside, then vanished into the shadows of the west side.

I pressed my fingers to the cold glass and whispered to no one, "You shouldn't have come back."

But she had.

And now I knew exactly where we'd be going tomorrow.

The Map Below

Morning came dressed in fog and guilt.
From my loft window, the museum looked more like a ghost than a landmark—half-shrouded, colorless, quietly daring anyone to notice it was still bleeding. The council vote from last night had changed everything; Maplewood's past had officially been sold to its own future. And somewhere inside that building, the truth was still locked behind the words Closed for Restoration.
Downstairs, the grinder's hum was my only sense of normal. Sam moved through the café like a commander of the mundane—refilling sugar bowls, wiping surfaces that didn't need wiping. When I entered, she handed me a mug. "You look like you slept on a conspiracy board."
"I didn't sleep," I said. "And technically it was a spreadsheet."
She frowned. "I can't tell if that's better or worse."
Liam arrived moments later with his laptop, two notebooks, and a camera strap slung across his chest. "Ready?"
"No," Sam said immediately. "You're not doing anything adventurous until you eat."
He smiled nervously, because he always smiled before doing something that scared him. "We're just looking. Daylight recon. That's all."
Sam looked at me. "Promise me."
I met her eyes and said, "We'll stay outside." It wasn't a lie—yet.

We crossed the square midmorning, the fog lifting just enough to reveal the museum's shape like a body under a sheet. The staff entrance was blocked by scaffolding, but the west lawn remained open. The air carried the smell of damp stone and something faintly metallic, like rain on old pennies.
"This is the spot," Liam said, pointing toward a vent low on the wall. "That's where the mystery camera was facing."
I crouched. The vent slats were bent, one corner pried loose. Rust had peeled away to show newer metal underneath. I ran my fingers lightly over the frame—cold, gritty, faintly damp.
"Smell that?" I asked.
He crouched beside me. "River mud."
"The tunnel," I said. "Someone's been through here."
He took photos from every angle, precise and methodical. "If they used this route, it's not just to hide evidence. It's to move it."
I nodded. "And they'd need a map."

He blinked. "A what?"

"Of the tunnels," I said. "Old construction records, city archives, maybe even blueprints. If they sealed the entrance decades ago, there has to be paperwork."

Liam's expression brightened in that I-can-Google-my-way-to-trouble sort of way. "City Hall still has public access terminals for permits. If I pull the museum's original foundation plans, maybe we'll see the tunnel's path."

"You're going to hack City Hall?" I asked, half amused, half worried.

"It's not hacking," he said. "It's politely reading things the mayor forgot to password-protect."

"Be careful," I said. "Politeness has limits."

Back at the café, Sam had turned the morning rush into an art form. Beans sat perched on the pastry case, eyes narrowed like he was supervising morale. When we slipped behind the counter, Sam gave us both the patented I-know-you're-up-to-something stare.

"Don't say it," I said.

"I wasn't going to," she said. "But if you vanish again, I'm putting an AirTag in your apron."

Liam set up at our side table and opened his laptop. He worked fast, fingers tapping lightly. After a few minutes, he whistled low. "Got it."

He spun the screen toward me. The city archives website flickered open, displaying a set of scanned blueprints from 1932. Underneath the museum's grid was a narrow line stretching westward toward the river. Service Tunnel—Water Drainage Access.

I leaned closer. "Look at that curve. It passes right under the old warehouse."

"The one rumored to be for sale," he said. "If Grant's project includes that property, she could use the tunnel to move things—artifacts, drives, whatever—without public record."

"And no one would question why the sub-basement's sealed," I said. "It's perfect."

He zoomed in on the lower annotation. "There's a symbol here—a little diamond near the tunnel's midpoint. Probably an access hatch. The map labels it Utility Shaft B."

"Utility Shaft," I repeated. "That's halfway between the museum and the river. The perfect handoff point."

Sam placed a cup beside me. "You two sound like you're narrating a bad spy movie."

"Except our villain wears pearls," I said.

The bell chimed and Mrs. Pickles entered with a flourish that defied weather or reason. She carried a rolled-up poster and three of her cats' whiskers in a sealed envelope. "For luck," she said.
"Why do I get the feeling this involves séances?" I asked.
She unrolled the poster—a faded tourist map of Maplewood from the 1950s, edges frayed and corners smudged. "My late husband collected these. It shows every old building. Including this."
Her finger landed on a small symbol near the river: Old Service Entrance.
"Right there," she said. "The cats knocked this down from a shelf this morning. Clearly, the universe wants you to find something."
"Or your cats like gravity," I said, but my pulse was already quickening. The mark matched the diamond on Liam's blueprint. Different eras, same location.
"You're incredible," I said, and Mrs. Pickles practically glowed. "But don't tell the cats. They'll demand royalties."
"Too late," she said. "They've opened a trust fund."

By noon, the museum had opened its doors to select maintenance staff—mostly uniformed workers and one bored guard. We watched from the café window as they hauled boxes into the west corridor.
"Rangel said he'd call if they found anything," Liam said, checking his phone. "So far, nothing."
"Which means we keep following the map," I said. "Quietly."
Sam set down her cloth and gave me that look again. "Quietly," she repeated. "Not illegally."
"Ish," I said.
She pointed her cloth like a sword. "You can't just add *ish* and make crimes optional."
But the truth was, curiosity had already signed its contract.

At three, a low whistle from Liam snapped me out of my espresso haze. "Look."
He held up his phone. A new email, from a sender with no name, no subject. Just a single attachment and one line of text: "If you want Barlow, follow the map."
My skin prickled. "Who sent it?"

He shook his head. "No signature. No metadata either—someone scrubbed it."

The attachment opened to a grainy scan of an old museum floorplan, marked in red ink. A line snaked from the Index Room down through a hidden stairwell labeled Storage Access, then curved toward the same tunnel on our blueprint. A small X sat near the diamond symbol.

"That's our utility shaft," I said. "But this version labels it differently—'Archivist's Passage.'"

"Barlow was the archivist," Liam said quietly.

"He drew this," I said. "Or someone did for him."

Sam leaned over the counter, studying the map. "This is how he escaped."

"Or how he meant to," I said. "If he got trapped down there…"

Liam swallowed. "We have to tell Rangel."

I nodded, but something in me resisted waiting. "He won't move without evidence. He needs probable cause, not hunches and maps from ghosts."

"Then we find evidence," Liam said.

At sunset, the square filled with soft amber light, the kind that makes even secrets look harmless. The museum's facade glowed like an old painting. I pulled my jacket tight, my pulse matching the clock tower's rhythm. Sam locked the café and pressed the spare key into my hand.

"Don't make me regret this," she said.

"I'll bring it back," I said.

"Bring you back," she corrected.

Liam adjusted his camera strap. "We'll stay in the open. If we can reach the river end of the tunnel, we might see where it's blocked. We're not going inside."

"Yet," I said.

"Please don't add yet to things," he said.

The river path was quieter than usual, just the faint sound of water folding over rocks and the buzz of insects too stubborn to accept autumn. The warehouse loomed ahead, its corrugated siding catching the light in sharp angles. A For Sale sign leaned against the fence, half-buried in weeds.

We followed the fence until we reached the back, where the old service entrance should have been. The ground sloped downward into a concrete recess filled with debris—planks, leaves, and a collapsed grate.

"There," Liam said softly, pointing to a metal door, half-hidden under ivy. It bore a faded stencil: Municipal Access — Authorized Personnel Only.

He crouched, brushed away grime, and found a padlock snapped clean. Not cut with bolt cutters—snapped, as if forced open from the inside. "Someone's been here," he said.

Inside the gap, a narrow tunnel disappeared into darkness. Air drifted out—damp, stale, tinged with oil and something older.

"Flashlight," I said, and he handed me his phone.

We shone the beam down the tunnel. Twenty feet in, the light caught a metal cabinet, half-open. Paper fluttered inside, faintly damp. One sheet clung to the edge, its header still legible:

MAPLEWOOD CULTURAL TRUST — FINANCIAL RECORDS

"Records," I breathed. "He hid them down here."

Liam reached carefully, fingers brushing the top page. It tore away in his hand. On the back, faint writing in pencil:

'IR–28 led here. If you're reading this, it's not just about money.'

"Barlow," I whispered.

Liam's voice was tight. "We have to go."

He was right. The sun had dropped; the river gleamed like steel. I tucked the page into my notebook, heart pounding.

As we turned to leave, a sound echoed from inside the tunnel—a faint scrape of shoe on stone. Then another. Slow, deliberate.

We froze. The light trembled in my hand. For a heartbeat, the tunnel stayed black. Then a new light flared deeper within—small, white, steady.

Someone else was down there.

We backed away slowly, steps silent on damp concrete, until we were clear of the recess. I pressed my back to the fence, breath thin, adrenaline clawing at my ribs.

Liam whispered, "They followed the map too."

"Or they never left," I said.

From the tunnel's mouth, the light vanished.

We ran.

Back at Brewed Awakening, Sam locked the door behind us before we could speak. Beans hopped onto the counter, tail twitching like a metronome.

"What happened?" she demanded.

I set the torn page on the table. "Proof," I said. "Barlow hid the museum's financial records in the tunnel. Someone tried to burn the rest."

Liam swallowed. "Someone's still down there."

Sam went pale. "Tell Rangel."

"I will," I said. "In the morning."

"Why not now?"

"Because whoever's down there is watching us tonight," I said. "And I'd rather they think we're still guessing."

Outside, fog crept back across the square, curling around lampposts like it had secrets to deliver. Inside, we watched the alley feed flicker once, then clear.

And in that single second of static, before the image returned, I swore I saw a face in the vent reflection—watching us back.

A Whistle and a Warning

Sleep and I barely shook hands that night. Every time I closed my eyes, I saw that flash of white light in the tunnel—the small circle of illumination that didn't belong to me.
When dawn finally pried open the sky, I gave up on pretending and went downstairs.
The café smelled like coffee and steel nerves. Sam was already there, tying her apron with brisk, surgical precision. Liam sat at the corner table, laptop open, face lit by the pale glow of surveillance footage.
"You didn't sleep either," I said.
He didn't look up. "Didn't want to miss anything."
The alley camera feed rolled quietly across the screen. For hours—nothing but fog and shadows. Then, at 2:14 a.m., a shape cut across the frame—slight, quick, head down. The light caught a museum badge clipped to a jacket. A worker. Or someone pretending to be one.
"Maintenance uniform," Liam murmured. "Heading toward the square, not the museum."
"And carrying something," I said. "See the weight in his shoulders? That's not a stroll."
Sam set down two mugs like offerings to the gods of poor decisions. "Please tell me you're showing this to Rangel."
"I texted him already," Liam said. "No response."
"Probably sleeping," Sam said. "Like normal people."
I blew on my coffee. "Normal left town when someone dropped keys under our door."

By eight, the café buzzed again—half customers, half curiosity seekers. Maplewood's tragedy had become its breakfast topic. The mayor's face smiled from the local paper, framed by the headline COUNCIL MOVES FORWARD WITH HOPE. Hope, in Maplewood, was just another way of saying we're ignoring something dangerous.
Mabel arrived with gossip, Mrs. Pickles with prophecies, and both settled in like furniture.
"Have you heard?" Mabel whispered. "The museum hired private security. Men in dark jackets, no patches. One nearly tripped over my pug."
"Justice at work," I said.
"They said they're inventorying the basement," she went on. "But the museum's closed. What kind of inventory happens behind locked doors?"

"The profitable kind," Sam muttered.

Before I could answer, the doorbell jingled again—and this time, it wasn't one of our regulars. A man stood there in a gray maintenance uniform, cap pulled low, tool bag in hand. His nametag read T. Anders.

"Coffee to go," he said, glancing around. His voice was rough, like gravel under a tire.

"Sure," I said, already pouring. "You're new?"

"Just started," he said. "Temporary assignment. Museum contractor."

Every cell in my body went on alert.

Liam, behind the counter, froze mid-type. "How's that project going?" he asked casually.

The man's eyes flicked toward him, calculating. "Lots of cleanup. Messy place. You folks see anything strange this week?"

I smiled the smile that hides knives. "Define strange."

He took the cup, left exact change, and walked out without a word. Through the window, I watched him cross the square—not toward the museum, but down the side street leading to the river path.

Sam exhaled. "He was fishing."

"Yeah," I said. "And I think we just took the bait."

At ten, my phone buzzed. Unknown Number. Again.

I answered. "This better not be another safety tip from a ghost."

A low voice rasped, "You were at the tunnel."

I stopped breathing. "Who is this?"

"Get rid of the page," it said. "You're in over your head."

"Who are you?" I repeated.

"Someone who doesn't want another body pulled from the river."

The line went dead.

Liam had been watching my face. "That was not your mother," he said.

"No," I said. "And they knew about the page."

I pulled the torn record Barlow had left from my notebook. The words stared up at me: 'If you're reading this, it's not just about money.' I didn't know what that meant yet, but whoever called me clearly did.

"Maybe we should hand that to Rangel," Liam said. "He's the one with a badge."

"He also works under the council," I said. "If Grant's pulling strings, he might not even know who he can trust."

Sam pinched the bridge of her nose. "Then we trust no one. And you stop answering anonymous calls."

By noon, the museum's facade was crawling with contractors—white vans, hard hats, clipboards. It looked less like a crime scene and more like a cover story wearing a safety vest.

Liam and I stepped out to grab lunch from the bakery across the street, just for a break from our own four walls. On our way back, a figure stepped from the alley beside the florist—nervous, shifting weight from foot to foot. The museum's young volunteer, Ethan.

"Miss Calder?" he said, eyes darting. "You need to hear this."

He looked over his shoulder, like the air behind him might have ears.

"Pike wasn't supposed to be there that night. His shift ended at ten. But he came back at eleven because someone called him."

"Who?" I asked.

"I don't know," he said. "But he told Barlow he got an anonymous text—said there was a leak in the west corridor. When he went, the lights went out. I saw Trent going in after him."

My heart clenched. "You're sure?"

He nodded. "He carried a flashlight and gloves. The kind you use for electrical work. Pike never came out."

"Why are you telling me this?" I asked.

"Because I'm afraid I could be next," he whispered.

And then someone shouted his name.

Ethan flinched, color draining from his face. Across the street, the maintenance man— T. Anders stood near a van, waving a clipboard.

"You've got deliveries piling up!" he called.

"I have to go," Ethan said, backing away. "Please—be careful."

He jogged toward the van, head down. The man clapped him on the shoulder, too firmly, then steered him inside. The doors closed, and the van pulled away, tires squealing slightly on the cobblestones.

Liam's voice was small. "That wasn't a delivery truck."

"No," I said. "That was a warning."

Back in the café, we pretended to function better than we really were. Sam handled customers. I wiped already-clean counters. Liam scrolled through city permit records until his hands shook.

At three, my phone buzzed again—this time a message, not a call. No number. Just a photo.

It was Ethan.

Taken from across the river, blurred but clear enough to show him standing beside the same van, eyes wide. The timestamp read twenty minutes ago.

A second message followed: "You're next."
I turned the screen toward Liam. His mouth went dry. "That's… specific."
Sam caught the look and froze. "What now?"
"Now," I said, "we stop waiting for permission."

At dusk, the square emptied of tourists. The museum sat quiet again, its windows glowing faintly. The air smelled like rain, one of those nights where the whole sky displays what it's thinking.
We waited until the contractors packed up. When the last van rolled off, we crossed the square toward the museum's west side, following the sound of our own bad ideas.
The maintenance vent gleamed faintly under the lamplight. Liam knelt beside it, prying carefully at the loosened corner. A faint whistling sound rose from within—soft, rhythmic, not mechanical.
He froze. "You hear that?"
I leaned closer. The sound wasn't wind. It was a low, tremulous whistle—human, breathy, repeated in uneven intervals.
"Someone's down there," I said.
He switched on his phone light and aimed it through the slats. The beam caught a flicker of movement—then a glint of brass. Something small lay wedged in the vent's grate.
"Hold this," he said, passing me the light. He used his pocket screwdriver to pry it free. A tiny metal whistle dropped into his palm, dented, stamped with letters: MAPLEWOOD YOUTH EXHIBIT — 1998.
Barlow's department. He used to give those out to visiting students.
"Clue or coincidence?" Liam asked.
"Both," I said. "It's always both."
Behind us, a faint click echoed—a door latch from the alley side. We spun around.
The maintenance man from the café stood in the half-light, arms crossed, expression unreadable.
"You shouldn't be here," he said.
"And you shouldn't be following us," I shot back.
His gaze flicked to the whistle in Liam's hand. "You think you're saving someone. You're not."
Before we could respond, a voice shouted from behind him. "Police! Hands where I can see them!"
Rangel.

The man bolted toward the river. Rangel chased, his flashlight beam slicing through the dark. Liam started to follow, but I grabbed his arm.
"No. Let him."
We watched as their shadows disappeared into the fog. The whistle trembled in Liam's fingers.
"What now?" he asked quietly.
"Now," I said, staring down the empty alley, "we figure out who's really giving the warnings."
Because in Maplewood, danger didn't come from strangers. It came from the people who already knew your coffee order.

Breaking the Silence

Fog hung over Maplewood like a secret kept too long. By the time I unlocked the café at six, my head was pounding with the echo of last night: the man in the maintenance cap, Rangel's shout, the flashlights slicing the river mist, and that small brass whistle in Liam's trembling hand stamped MAPLEWOOD YOUTH EXHIBIT — 1998.
I brewed the first pot like it might explain anything. It didn't.
Sam arrived in her cardigan armor, hair in a no-nonsense knot that said try me. Liam slipped in right behind her, eyes shadowed, laptop bag bumping his knee.
"Rangel texted at four," he said, voice low. "They lost him near the river. The fog swallowed footprints, and the cameras down there are… theoretical."
"Welcome to Maplewood," Sam muttered.
The whistle lay on a napkin beside the register like a relic with a headache. I nudged it with one finger. "Barlow left it. Or someone who wanted us to think that."
"Could be both," Liam said. "He used to hand them out to school tours. Said kids listened better when they had something to hold."
"He wasn't wrong," I said, picturing a dozen fourth-graders clutching identical whistles and promising with the sincerity of soda-fueled youth never to blow them indoors.
The door chime saved me from sentiment. Mrs. Pickles swept in with perfume and purpose, three of her cats' whiskers sealed in a coin envelope like a talisman.
"You're early," I said, pouring her tea.
"The Triumvirate woke me at five," she said. "They were staring at the toaster."
"Harbinger of doom?" Sam asked.
"Carbs," Mrs. Pickles said, then leaned in. "But also doom."
Mabel Cho arrived two beats later, breathless, phone in hand. "Breaking: City Hall posted a notice at dawn. The museum will conduct an 'archive deaccession and mold remediation' tomorrow morning—closed to the public, staff only."
"Mold remediation," Sam repeated flatly. "In winter."
"They're going to burn something," I said. "Again."
Mabel nodded like a priest. "The notice uses the phrase 'damaged inventory purge.' That's grant-speak for 'the stuff that could indict us is suddenly too fuzzy to read.'"

I felt the caffeine hit my bloodstream like resolve. "Then today we stop whispering in our own heads."

"How?" Liam asked.

"By creating a record they can't just purge," I said. "We put everything we have in one place—dates, times, photos, the wristband, the key, the clips of Grant and Trent, the vent, the tunnel, the whistle, the assistant's statement. We copy it five different ways and stash it five different places. If anything happens to one of us, the rest of it survives."

Sam slid a legal pad across the counter. "Say it with me: lists are love."

I smiled despite the thrum in my ribs. "Lists are love."

We worked between orders, the three of us moving like a small orchestra. Liam set up at table two with his laptop, compiling footage and timestamps. Sam toggled the front of house with running interference—extra napkins, fewer questions, the kind of barista patter that can turn a mob into a line. I stood at the pass-through window with a pen and our case in messy ink.

TIMELINE:

Two nights pre-gala, 9:42 p.m. — Grant and Trent on our alley camera moving boxes from the museum toward Main Street.

Gala night, 11:50 to 12:10 a.m. — Museum Wi-Fi blackout.

11:57 p.m. — Gift shop receipt, initials O.P. (Pike) — alive before midnight.

Just after midnight — Silent secondary sensor trip; lobby alarm never sounded.

A few hours later — Wristband (staff gray) found behind our café with river mud; broken camera hinge by our dumpster.

Morning after — Burned folders labeled Donor Archives in West Maintenance corridor; crates warm.

Council vote — Emergency redevelopment passes, giving Grant control of museum property.

Tunnel — Blueprints and vintage map confirm service tunnel from museum to river warehouse; Utility Shaft B marked halfway.

Anonymous email — "If you want Barlow, follow the map."

River entrance — Door forced from inside; we find a financial record page with Barlow's note: "It's not just about money."

Night — Unknown maintenance man (T. Anders) fishes at our counter; later spots us at vent; Rangel gives chase; suspect escapes.

Dawn notice — Archive purge scheduled for tomorrow morning.

Underneath, I added the through-lines that felt less like facts and more like bones:

Pike lured back with fake text about a leak; confronted Trent over the drives.

Barlow hiding with evidence; used whistle and map as breadcrumbs.

Grant's corridor isn't security—it's a laundering machine for land and records.

Someone inside the system is feeding us clues and watching us.

"Add Ethan," Sam said softly. "Volunteer. Witness. In danger."

I wrote his name in the corner and circled it. The circle looked too much like a target.

By midmorning, the café settled into a rhythm that might have been peaceful if not for the sense that the floor was moving under us. Mrs. Pickles organized a spontaneous knitting circle by the window, which somehow became a rumor distribution hub with yarn. Mabel offered "pro bono PR advice" to the entire room. Through it all, Liam built our case with careful hands and redundant backups.

"Okay," he said finally, tapping the screen. "I'm sending you both an encrypted copy. Password is—"

"Not our cat's name," Sam said.

He blinked. "It's not."

"Good," she said. "Because Beans would sell us out for a sardine."

As if hearing his cue, Beans leapt onto the counter and sat directly on my legal pad, tail a metronome of indifference. I slid him three inches left and pretended I was in control of my own life.

The door chimed. Officer Rangel stepped in, a windblown crease between his brows deep enough to lose loose change in. He accepted coffee he hadn't yet ordered and gestured toward the back.

"We're not hiding," I said.

"I've got fifteen minutes and a headache," he said. "Talk."

I told him everything—the whistle, the tunnel note, the river entrance forced from inside, the "mold remediation" notice, Ethan's warning, the maintenance man who keeps appearing where he shouldn't.

He listened the way only small-town detectives do—quiet, deliberate. "We found more burned folders in the west corridor," he said when I finished. "Smelled like accelerant. Someone's cleaning house with a match."

"Before the purge makes it legal," I said.

He nodded once. "We also found a metal shard near the old vault—looked like part of a key bow. Lab says it's from the same series as your West Maintenance key."

I pulled our bagged fragment from the drawer. "We found the other half by the vent last night."

He took it, studied the jagged edge, and very carefully didn't look surprised. "These fit," he said. "We'll test them officially."

"Is Ethan safe?" I asked.

Rangel's mouth tightened. "We're trying to locate him."

"Meaning you can't," I said quietly.

"Meaning we're trying harder," he said. "And before you ask—no, I don't know who your maintenance friend is. The name T. Anders doesn't match any contractor on file. We've got eyes on the river approaches and the west corridor. But I can't close half a town for a hunch."

"It's more than a hunch," I said, the whistle cold in my palm.

"I know," he said. "Do me a favor, Calder."

"If you say stop, I'm going to lie to you."

"Then here's one you can keep," he said. "If someone texts you a meeting place, don't go. Send it to me. And—" he glanced at the alley monitor— "keep that door locked."

He left with the key fragment and a cup he didn't have time to drink. The empty doorway felt like a missing stair.

The lull between late breakfast and early lunch became our planning hour. Liam finished the master packet and wrote five hiding spots on a sticky note in tidy block letters:

1. USB in flour bin
2. SD card taped under register
3. Copy on my laptop (encrypted)
4. Printed summary in Sam's office binder
5. Email draft to journalist (unsent)

"Who's the journalist?" Sam asked.

"An old classmate," Liam said. "Works two towns over. Not flashy, but honest."

"We don't hit send unless we have to," I said. "But we might have to."

We all looked at the fifth line like it was a fire alarm covered in glass.

At noon, a school group marched past holding maps like explorers. My stomach twisted imagining Barlow handing out whistles to kids in this very lobby. Listen; look; be gentle with the past. He'd said a version of that to me when I was sixteen and cataloging donor file numbers for extra cash.

Listen; look; be gentle with the past.

The door chimed—two men in matching dark jackets, no insignia, radiating the polite menace of private security. They ordered black coffees, took them to a corner table, and made a show of ignoring the room.

"They're not from here," Mabel whispered, appearing at my elbow. "They hold cups like props."

"What are they watching?" I asked.

She didn't have to answer. The men's eyes slid to Liam's open laptop, to the alley monitor, to the bulletin board where we posted bake sale notices and missing cat posters. Their gaze lingered on my legal pad even though Beans was sitting on it.

"Good," I said lightly to Beans. "You're finally useful."

He blinked. I took it as agreement.

The men left after fifteen minutes with cups still full. A minute later, my phone buzzed on the counter. Unknown number. Text only.

LOOK WHERE YOU SHOULDN'T. THEY'LL LOOK WHERE YOU DO.

"What does that even mean?" Sam asked, peering over my shoulder.

"It means we're being watched," I said. "And whoever sent that thinks they're on our side."

"Or they want you to think that," Sam said.

"Both," Liam murmured. We'd started using both as a verb.

I texted the screenshot to Rangel with a single line: Friends or theater?

He replied: Assume theater. Wear a seatbelt.

By late afternoon, the square's winter light flattened into gray. I wiped already-clean tables again and tried to line up my breath with the clock tower's steady swing. Tomorrow's purge ticked louder in my head than the hands above the museum.

"Okay," I said finally. "We're done being reactive."

Sam raised an eyebrow. "You have a plan?"

"Something between bold and reckless," I said. "We split up—briefly. Sam stays here. Liam and I take two routes. I'll visit City Hall and politely read donor filings for the museum's land titles. Liam, you do a slow lap of the square and see who follows. If anyone shadows you, you come back. If no one does, you meet me in the records room with croissants and a smile."

"And if this is a terrible idea?" Sam asked.

"Then we have croissants," I said.

She stared, then sighed, then handed me my coat. "Fifteen minutes. AirTag in your pocket."

"You didn't," I said.

She did. Of course she did.

City Hall's records room smelled like paper and floor wax and retirement. The clerk at the desk looked up, recognized me, and brightened. "Looking for land records?"

"Specifically the museum's west wing parcels and any development holds attached to the Heritage Corridor," I said.

He handed me a key to drawer B-14, which did nothing for my pulse. I pulled folders, scanned dates, wrote numbers. The paper trail was a river with bends: donor trusts, holding companies, a shell that pointed to another shell that pointed to an address that didn't exist. A signature jumped the page—D. GRANT—not on a sale, but on a temporary stewardship clause that surrendered the museum's decision-making power to the council after a "security event."

"Security event," I muttered. "How convenient."

My phone buzzed. Liam: No tail. Walking by museum. You good?

Good. Bring croissant, I replied.

A shadow fell across the file. I looked up.

Councilwoman Dolores Grant.

She wore the same polished navy coat as yesterday and a smile that could turn rain to snow. "Hattie Calder," she said. "What a surprise."

"Public records are public," I said. "I like to read."

"Curiosity is a lovely trait," she said. "In moderation."

Her gaze flicked to the clause with her signature. "Old paperwork. Necessary in an emergency."

"Tragic how emergencies pop up on schedule," I said.

She stepped closer—not enough to threaten, just enough to be the weather. "Be careful," she said. "You run a lovely café. I'd hate to see it... struggle."

"Oh," I said sweetly. "Is that what we're calling arson threats now?"

She tilted her head, smile cracking. "You should leave policy to your betters," she said, and drifted away on a fog of expensive perfume.

"I don't have betters," I muttered. "I have sisters."

Liam appeared moments later with a paper bag and the exact smile I'd requested. "Please tell me you didn't make eye contact with anyone," he said.

"Only the councilwoman," I said, and ate a croissant out of spite.

Evening drew its curtain early. We flipped the OPEN sign to CLOSED and kept the lamps low, a homey glow against the square's chill. The private security men did another slow drive-by. I waved. They didn't wave back.

We gathered at the back table with our packet—the one Liam had built—open like a map. We added City Hall's clause, circled the tunnel's utility shaft, underlined tomorrow's purge notice. Then we did the one thing that felt like both risk and insurance: we printed a four-page Summary of Findings and slid it into a manila envelope addressed to Det. Rangel—CONFIDENTIAL with a sticky note: If we vanish, this is where to start digging.

"Dramatic," Sam said.

"Motivational," I said.

Beans hopped into the chair beside me and head-butted my arm hard enough to smear my pen line. "Subtle," I said.

We were closing up when the front bell rang once—soft, insistent. I glanced at the clock—8:19. We don't unlock after eight unless the world is on fire.

Liam checked the camera feed. A lone figure stood just outside, hood up, face shadowed. Not the maintenance man. Not Grant. Smaller. Still.

My phone buzzed. Unknown number. "Please. Two minutes. I have what he hid."

"Barlow?" Liam breathed.

I looked at the alley monitor, at the vent that had shown me a face for a fraction of a second. At the envelope for Rangel. At the whistle on the napkin.

"Witnesses," Sam said, already moving to the door. "Eyes up. Locks ready."

I nodded, slid the chain to its catch, and cracked the door three inches.

A gaunt man stepped into the slice of light, eyes hollowed by too many nights in the wrong places. He lifted his hand. In it, a battered dictaphone. Old. Scuffed. Real.

"Please," he said, voice a rasp I knew from the museum's quiet halls. "Don't let them burn this."

"Dr. Barlow," I said.

His knees buckled.

We caught him before he hit the floor.

And somewhere outside—in the square where Maplewood pretends not to listen—a car engine turned over once and idled.

The Dictaphone

For a man who'd been missing for nearly a week, Dr. Fred Barlow still smelled faintly of peppermint tea and museum dust. He was thinner, paler, shaking under a coat that looked like it had lost the same number of days he had. We lowered him gently onto the couch in the café's back room. Sam grabbed a blanket, Liam a glass of water, and I pulled the blinds until the only light came from the soft lamps near the espresso machine.

He blinked at us like we were part of a dream he hadn't decided to trust.
"You kept the place open," he rasped.
"Someone had to," I said. "You've been busy disappearing."
"Not disappearing," he said. "Preserving." His hand tightened around the battered dictaphone. "This is everything they didn't want you to hear."
Liam crouched beside him. "You're safe here, Dr. Barlow."
"No one is safe," he whispered. "Not when history belongs to the highest bidder."

He slept for almost an hour, head tilted toward the sound of Beans purring near his knee. Sam stood guard at the door with the poise of someone who'd spent her whole life managing chaos with caffeine. Liam sat beside the small recorder like it might evaporate. When Barlow stirred, I poured him a weak tea and waited for his eyes to focus.
"They killed Owen," he said quietly, not as an accusation but a confession. "He found the duplicate drives. I told him to leave it alone."
"What was on them?" I asked.
He licked his lips. "The land transfers. The Heritage Corridor wasn't about preservation—it was about rezoning. Grant's donors bought parcels along the river years ago, but they needed the museum to fall under the council's jurisdiction. When the medallion theft distracted everyone, they used the chaos to sign over control of the west wing."
Liam frowned. "You mean the museum board gave up ownership?"
Barlow nodded. "Under the guise of a security emergency. I refused to sign. Trent brought the paperwork anyway. When Owen found the drives, they realized they'd left a digital trail. I told him to destroy them." His voice cracked. "He tried. He never made it home."
Sam's voice was steady, the way it is when she's one blink from breaking. "And you ran."
"They would've blamed me," he said. "The curator's signature was on every page. I hid what I could. The dictaphone was insurance. I recorded

everything—Grant's calls, Trent's threats, even the meeting where they planned the fake 'mold purge.' I left one copy in the Index Room, another near the tunnel. When I realized they were burning evidence, I took the last one and ran."

"You did the right thing," I said.

He looked at me, hollow-eyed. "The right thing still got a man killed."

Liam set up his laptop and carefully connected the recorder with an adapter. The old device crackled to life, static whispering like ghosts. Barlow's voice, younger and steadier, filled the room.

"Meeting minutes, October fifteenth," the recording began. "Present: Dolores Grant, Trent Morrow, finance representative 'R.S.'—unverified surname. Discussion: expedited development under the Maplewood Heritage Corridor Initiative…"

We listened in silence as Grant's voice slid through the static, honeyed and cold.

"Once we transfer the land use permits, the state grant doubles. The museum can be folded into the corridor's fiscal model. No one reads the fine print."

Then Trent: "And the security team?"

Grant again: "Let them think the theft was random. People love a scandal more than they love paperwork."

The recording hissed, popped, continued.

R.S. asked, "And Barlow?"

Grant's laugh was sharp. "He's sentimental. He'll come around, or he'll resign."

Barlow's recorded voice: "And if I don't?"

Trent: "Then we'll light a match under your history."

The file clicked and went silent. Liam hit pause. The hum of the espresso machine sounded suddenly enormous.

Sam exhaled first. "Well," she said. "That's arson. Conspiracy. Fraud."

"And motive," I said. "Enough to ruin careers."

"Enough to make them desperate," Barlow whispered. "You can't let them destroy the rest."

"They're doing the purge tomorrow," Liam said. "If we release this tonight—"

"They'll bury it before it trends," Sam said. "And if they think we have the file, they'll come for us next."

I looked at the little recorder, scuffed and humming faintly like it still had secrets. "Then we don't give it to anyone yet. We make it public at the same time we hand it to Rangel. If they try to suppress it, it'll already be out."

Barlow's hand trembled. "Do you trust him?"

I thought of Rangel's tired eyes and the way he always told the truth even when it made his job harder. "Enough to give him a chance."

We hid the dictaphone in an empty coffee tin and sealed it with tape. Sam labeled it "House Blend" in her neat handwriting and slid it onto the top shelf, right beside the emergency cocoa.

Liam wrote a script to auto-upload the recording to multiple sites at noon tomorrow—the same time the museum purge was scheduled. "Failsafe," he said. "If anything happens, the truth releases itself."

Barlow watched him work with a faint, wistful smile. "You remind me of myself once. Before the paperwork."

"Hope that's a compliment," Liam said.

"It is," Barlow murmured. "You still believe small actions matter."

"They do," I said. "It's just that the consequences drink black coffee."

That earned the faintest laugh, hoarse but real.

We let him rest again. Outside, the square was mostly empty, lamplight pooling gold across the cobblestones. Through the blinds, I saw a pair of dark SUVs park along the curb near the museum. Men in plain coats stepped out, one lifting a phone to his ear.

"Security or cleanup?" Sam asked.

"Both," I said.

At nine, Rangel texted. Short, clipped. "Stay inside. Movement at museum. Will update."

I sent back, "We have Barlow."

The typing dots appeared, vanished, reappeared. Then: "Keep him safe. Don't leave."

The café's quiet stretched long. We took turns checking the alley feed—nothing but fog and the usual flicker of passing headlights. Barlow stirred near midnight, coughing weakly.

"I thought Maplewood was small enough to be safe," he said. "But the thing about small towns—they fit lies in smaller boxes."

"You're safe now," I said, though my voice wasn't sure it believed it.

He reached into his coat pocket and pulled out a folded envelope, edges smudged and soft. "There's one more piece," he said. "My resignation letter. Never sent. It names every donor and every account Trent used to funnel payments. I didn't dare put it online. Too traceable."

He handed it to me. "You're better at hiding things than I am."

I took it gently. "We'll guard it."

"You won't have to for long," he whispered. "Once the world hears their voices, the rest will unravel."

Outside, the fog thickened again. The museum clock struck midnight, each chime echoing like a slow countdown.

Beans jumped onto the counter and stared toward the door. A moment later, headlights swept across the front windows—two vehicles, stopping without parking lights. The café's shadows stretched long and sharp.

Sam moved to the light switch. "Do we hide or fight?"

"Neither," I said. "We wait."

The car doors opened. Heavy steps on the cobblestones. Then, a sharp rap at the front door—two knocks, pause, one knock. Not random. A pattern.

Rangel's voice, muffled but calm. "It's me. Open up."

Sam exhaled and unlatched the chain. He stepped inside, rain dripping from his coat, eyes scanning the room before landing on Barlow. Relief flickered across his face.

"Thank God," he said. "We thought—well, doesn't matter. You found him."

"He found us," I said.

Rangel knelt beside Barlow. "You're safe now. I've got officers watching both exits."

Barlow's fingers twitched toward the recorder tin. "It's all there," he said. "Their voices. Their plan."

Rangel nodded. "We'll keep it secure."

Something in his tone made me pause—too even, too formal.

"Detective," I said slowly, "who's watching the museum right now?"

He hesitated. "A rotating team. Why?"

"Because if they're burning evidence tomorrow, someone's prepping it tonight."

He straightened. "I'll check it myself."

I handed him the envelope. "Barlow's resignation. It names donors. Make copies."

He took it carefully, eyes narrowing. "You trust me with this?"

"I'm out of better options," I said.

He smiled, thin but sincere. "That's all I ask."

He left as quietly as he'd come, locking the door behind him. We watched his taillights vanish toward the square.

Sam turned to me. "You think he'll actually file it?"
"I think he'll try," I said. "But he's playing against people who don't lose."

An hour passed. We started to breathe again. Liam dozed in the chair beside the monitor. Beans curled on his lap. Sam flipped through the ledger, pretending to read. I sat by the window, counting streetlights. Then, at 1:14 a.m., the phone on the counter rang once. Not the café line—the secure one we'd only given Rangel.
I answered. "Detective?"
Static. Then his voice, low and tight. "Hattie—leave the café. Now."
"What happened?"
"They knew," he said. "The purge isn't tomorrow. It's tonight."
The line went dead.
A sound cracked the quiet—the distant roar of engines. Down the street, headlights flared again, brighter this time, moving fast toward the square.
Sam's face went white. "They're coming here."
Barlow pushed himself up, unsteady. "Take the dictaphone. Run."
I grabbed the coffee tin from the shelf, tape still sealing its lid, and shoved it into Liam's backpack. "Out the back," I said. "We go through the alley, then the clock tower."
Sam locked the front door as the first engine revved outside. Tires skidded. Headlights spilled through the windows, turning the café gold and then red.
"Go," she said.
We ran for the back door. Behind us, the glass shuddered under the first blow.
Maplewood had stopped pretending not to listen.

Ashes Before Dawn

We burst into the alley behind Brewed Awakening just as the second crash shook the front windows. The sound of splintering glass echoed through the narrow lane, mixing with the clatter of garbage lids and the sharp hiss of steam from a vent pipe. My boots hit the wet pavement; my breath came in clouds. Behind me, Liam's backpack thumped with every step—the taped coffee tin inside knocking like a heartbeat we couldn't afford to lose.

"This way," Sam called, cutting across toward the old bakery delivery path that led uphill to the clock tower. She was faster than I expected, fury apparently a good fuel source. "They'll check the street first!"

We ducked behind the row of dumpsters. I risked a glance back. The café's glow was now fractured glass and chaos—dark figures moved inside, flashlights slicing through the fogged-up windows. They weren't police. They moved too smoothly, too organized. The kind of men who didn't ask questions, just cleaned up the ones already answered.

Liam stumbled beside me. "They're torching the place, aren't they?"

"Not yet," I said. "They're looking for the recorder."

"House Blend," Sam muttered. "Who knew that would be our most literal flavor."

We made it halfway to the square when a set of headlights cut across the side street, pinning us in sudden brightness. I yanked Liam down behind a stack of recycling bins; Sam froze beside me. The van rolled slowly past—one of the museum fleet vehicles, logo half peeled. The passenger side window slid down, and I saw Trent Morrow's profile lit by his phone screen, eyes sharp as coins.

Barlow's whisper came from behind us, breathless but certain. "That's him."

"You're supposed to be resting," I hissed.

"Rest later," he said. "Right now, I need to see where they go."

He was right. Trent wasn't heading toward Brewed Awakening. He turned uphill, toward the museum itself.

"They're not burning our café," Sam said softly. "They're finishing the purge."

The climb to the clock tower was a blur of brick and fog. We ducked into the narrow service door beneath the bell loft, the one only the local kids and delivery guys knew existed. It opened with a shove that left my shoulder throbbing. Inside smelled of oil, old wood, and forgotten time.

Liam dropped his bag gently on the floor. "Okay," he panted. "Game plan."

"Barlow and Sam stay here," I said. "You and I go to the museum."

Sam looked ready to argue, but Barlow caught her hand. "She's right. I can barely stand. But you'll need to record what happens tonight. They'll cover it by morning."

Liam hesitated, eyes flicking between us. "If they're burning files, we'll never get the data back."

"Then we stop them before they start," I said. "Or we take proof before they finish."

I pulled my phone. Rangel's text thread was empty—no new messages. My stomach dropped. "We're on our own."

Sam reached into her coat pocket and handed me the small silver key fragment we hadn't turned over to the detective. "You might need this more than he does."

I pocketed it. "Keep the tin safe. If anything happens—"

"Don't you dare finish that sentence," she snapped. "You're coming back."

Her voice cracked halfway through, and I pretended not to notice.

We followed the service path along the ridge overlooking the square. Maplewood's streets looked different from above—peaceful, quiet, almost too innocent. The museum's silhouette loomed at the far edge of the hill, its glass atrium glowing faintly like a lantern in fog. The main entrance was dark. But a dull orange flicker pulsed near the west maintenance wing.

"Please tell me that's not fire," Liam whispered.

"It's not supposed to be," I said. "But it probably is."

We crept closer, keeping to the hedge line. The scent of smoke reached us first—chemical, not wood. Two men in work jackets were wheeling crates toward a small furnace vent outside the west corridor, feeding in stacks of paper folders and snapping photographs of the ashes with a company tablet.

Trent supervised, sleeves rolled, face half-shadowed. He was shouting something over the wind.

"...all donor records before sunrise! And get that vault open!"

One of the men hesitated. "Council said—"

"Council doesn't matter," Trent barked. "They already got what they wanted."

I glanced at Liam. "Recording?"

He lifted his phone, camera light off, video rolling. "Got it."
Then, without warning, a different light swept across the courtyard—a flashlight beam slicing past us. We dove behind the railing as a third man appeared from the east wing entrance, walkie pressed to his mouth.
"Trent, we've got movement near the ridge."
Trent looked up, scanning the shadows. My pulse hammered so loud I was sure he'd hear it. For a moment his gaze swept over our hiding spot, then moved on. "Double it," he said. "No witnesses."
He disappeared back inside.
Liam mouthed, "We need to move."
"Not yet," I whispered. "One more minute."
Another crate hit the furnace, flames licking higher. Then a sound—a crack of metal—echoed from deeper in the wing. One of the men called out, "Sir! Something's jamming the vault door!"
I risked a look. The west corridor vault—half-open, half-melted—was sparking against its hinge. And in that flicker, I saw the glint of brass.
"The medallion," I breathed. "They didn't steal it—they hid it."
Liam frowned. "Why hide it here?"
"To make it look gone," I said. "They can claim the theft destroyed the proof of ownership. It's their reset button."
I started forward before I realized I'd moved. Liam grabbed my sleeve. "Hattie, don't—"
"Trust me," I said. "Just once."
We circled wide through the maintenance yard until we reached the vent opening. The furnace burned steady inside, but the ground around it was littered with discarded folders—some half-burnt, some damp from the fog. I crouched, scanning labels. Donor Archives. Parcel Transfer Agreements. Heritage Corridor Fund.
Liam knelt beside me, pulling a pair of tongs from his tool pouch—he'd never met a backpack he couldn't overprepare. "Grab what's legible."
We filled his bag with every intact sheet we could reach, sealing them inside a plastic sleeve. Then, as we turned to go, the crackle of a radio froze us.
"…movement confirmed west vent. Two targets. Orders?"
"Secure them," Trent's voice said.
Liam mouthed, "Run."

The chase through the museum grounds was a blur of boots on gravel and flashlight beams cutting through mist. I could hear the men shouting—short, clipped orders, not the chaos of amateurs. Liam stayed close, clutching the bag like his own pulse depended on it. We ducked behind the marble fountain near the old courtyard. The museum bell tolled one— a lonely, echoing note.

Footsteps pounded closer. A flashlight beam swept past the fountain's edge. Liam's breath came ragged. I reached into my pocket, fingers closing around the silver key fragment. My heart dropped when I realized what I was about to do.

"Stay down," I whispered.

Before he could argue, I darted out from behind the fountain, straight into the beam's glare. "Hey!" I shouted. "Looking for someone?"

The nearest guard froze. His partner swung the light toward me, momentary confusion giving me just enough of an edge. I hurled the key fragment as hard as I could into the hedgerow across the courtyard. It hit metal with a sharp clang.

"There!" one shouted, pivoting toward the sound.

I bolted in the opposite direction, Liam at my heels before I even heard him move. We sprinted across the cobblestones and back up toward the ridge trail, the sound of shouting and radios chasing us until it all blurred into the fog.

We didn't stop until we reached the clock tower again. Sam yanked open the service door as soon as she saw us. "You're bleeding," she said. "What happened?"

I looked down. A shallow cut along my forearm, streaked with ash. "Souvenir."

Barlow sat up when he saw the bag. "You went back."

"We had to," I said. "Trent's burning the records tonight. We got what we could."

Liam set the bag on the floor and opened it. The smell of smoke filled the small space. He pulled out the folder on top—edges singed, label barely intact. Sam leaned in to read it.

Heritage Corridor Fund — Beneficiary Accounts.

Barlow exhaled. "That's it."

Sam flipped it open. "Half of this is redacted."

"Half is enough," I said. "We just need to connect the signatures."

Liam rubbed his temple. "We should upload this to the failsafe along with the recording."

Barlow nodded. "Do it before dawn. By morning, this will be over one way or another."

Outside, the eastern sky was paling—the first thread of dawn seeping through the fog. Down below, the museum's windows glowed with that faint, unnatural orange that said the fire was still eating its secrets. Sirens began to wail in the distance—maybe the fire department, maybe something worse.

Liam hit the final upload command. "Scheduled. Noon release. Everything we've got."

Sam stood at the narrow window, arms crossed. "What now?"

I looked toward the burning museum and the waking town below. "Now we see if Maplewood remembers how to tell the truth."

Barlow's voice was faint, almost tender. "And if it doesn't?"

"Then we remind it," I said.

Somewhere below, the first siren cut off suddenly, the sound swallowed by the fog.

Morning had come to Maplewood—but it smelled like smoke.

The Fire Beneath the Glass

The fire engines reached the museum just after sunrise. From the clock tower, we watched their lights flicker like pulsebeats through the thinning fog. Smoke rose steady and thin—too neat for a true accident. I'd seen enough campfires to know when someone wanted something to burn and still look innocent.
Barlow stood beside me at the window, his coat draped over his shoulders like the shell of an old soldier. "They'll call it an electrical short," he said. "Old wiring. Poor maintenance. The perfect scapegoat."
"They always do," I said.
Down below, firefighters hauled hoses across the courtyard, spraying what was left of the west wing. Even from this distance, I could see the way Trent barked orders at them, directing them away from the archive rooms and toward areas that were already charred beyond recognition.
Sam appeared behind us with a thermos and four mugs. "Coffee," she said. "Because running on fear alone isn't sustainable."
Liam took a mug and sat on the floor, laptop open on his knees. "Failsafe's still queued. The file will post automatically in five hours. But once it's live, they'll know we're the source."
Barlow gave a small nod. "Good. That means it worked."
I sipped the bitter coffee, eyes still on the burning glass of the museum atrium. "Good is relative."

By midmorning, Maplewood Square was buzzing with police tape and local reporters. Mabel Cho had her phone out before the fire chief even started his briefing, narrating a live feed for her gossip circle. "Historic loss," she said, her voice appropriately mournful. "Possible foul play. But the real story—who benefits?"
"That woman is both the problem and the solution," Sam muttered.
We kept our distance. Too many uniforms, too many questions. Rangel hadn't texted back since last night. That silence felt heavy, the kind that comes when someone knows more than they're allowed to say.
At ten, Liam's screen pinged. A message from the encrypted account he'd set up for the uploads. Received inquiry: file flagged as pending legal review.
He swore under his breath. "Someone's already intercepting it."
"Can they stop it?" I asked.
"Not unless they shut down half the server farm. But they can delay the public post."

"Meaning we've got a few hours to stay invisible," Sam said. "After that, we're either heroes or suspects."
"Probably both," I said.

We decided to move Barlow before the police decided to 'question' him again. The old janitor's house by the river had been empty for months; Barlow still had the keys. He insisted it was safer there. "No one checks what they've already forgotten," he said.
By the time we reached the riverbank, the sun had burned through the fog. The house sat slumped beside the bridge, windows boarded, roof mossed over. Liam pried the side door open with a screwdriver.
"Charming," Sam said. "In a haunted kind of way."
Inside smelled of damp paper and rust. Barlow found a chair and sank into it like the air had weight. "Everything I tried to protect ended up ash," he murmured.
"Not everything," I said. "You're still here. The recording's safe. The files will go public."
He looked at me with tired eyes. "You still think truth fixes things."
"Don't you?"
He smiled faintly. "Once, yes. Before I learned how easily people trade it for comfort."
Outside, a car door slammed. Sam froze, motioning toward the window. A black sedan idled on the bridge, tinted windows rolled up. It wasn't a police cruiser.
"They followed us," Liam whispered.
Barlow's hand tightened on the chair arm. "Not Grant. Her fixer."
"How do you know?"
"Because he always drives alone."

We ducked behind the curtain as the car door opened. A tall man stepped out, dark coat, gloves, expressionless. He scanned the area, then turned toward the riverbank path. In his hand, he carried a small black case.
Liam whispered, "He's got a signal jammer."
I cursed under my breath. "They're tracing the upload. He's here to block it."
"Then we move," Sam said, already reaching for Barlow's arm. "Back door, now."
We slipped out through the kitchen into the back lot. The path wound along the river toward the pedestrian bridge that led back to town. Liam checked his phone. "No signal. He's close."

We reached the midpoint of the bridge before I dared to glance back. The man in black stood at the far end, phone to his ear, eyes on us. Then he started walking.
Liam's fingers flew across his phone screen. "I can boost the signal manually if we hit open air."
"You've got sixty seconds," Sam said.
Barlow clutched my arm. "If he catches us—"
"He won't," I said, though my pulse disagreed.
Liam stopped at the railing and raised his phone skyward. "Almost—there!" A single bar flickered to life. He hit SEND on the mirror file.
The man broke into a run.
Liam shoved the phone into his pocket. "It's out!"
"Then we run," I said.
We sprinted across the bridge, wind slicing our faces. Sam was the first to reach the other side; she threw open the maintenance gate. I turned just in time to see the man halt midspan, hand pressed to his earpiece. His voice carried faintly over the wind: "It's too late. They've uploaded it."
He didn't chase us. He just stood there, staring after us, until we disappeared into the streets.

By the time we reached the square again, Maplewood was chaos. The news vans had arrived, crowding the police perimeter. The fire was mostly out, leaving behind a blackened shell and columns of smoke twisting into a bright blue sky. Reporters swarmed every witness, shouting questions about corruption, fraud, missing files.
Mabel spotted us from across the street and gasped. "You three again! Wait—you were there last night, weren't you? What do you know?"
"Nothing," Sam said quickly. "We just serve coffee."
"Right," Mabel said, already typing. "And apparently serve breaking news now, too."
Liam grabbed my sleeve. "Look."
Across the street, Councilwoman Grant stood before the cameras, her expression solemn. "This is a tragedy for our town," she was saying. "The Maplewood Museum has long been a pillar of our community. We will cooperate fully with investigators to determine the cause."
She looked composed—too composed. But for the first time since I'd met her, there was a faint tremor in her hand as she adjusted the microphone.
"Think she's seen the upload yet?" Sam asked.
"Not yet," I said. "But she will."

At noon exactly, every phone in Maplewood buzzed. The recording of Grant's voice filled the air—on social media feeds, news alerts, even the town radio station. Her calm, calculated tone speaking of "expedited development" and "letting people love a scandal more than paperwork." The square went still.

Grant froze mid-sentence. Reporters shouted. Cameras pivoted. Somewhere in the crowd, someone laughed—short, disbelieving, triumphant.

Rangel's cruiser pulled up to the curb. He climbed out, eyes meeting mine across the chaos. Relief and exasperation warred on his face. "You couldn't wait, could you?"

"Apparently not," I said.

He sighed. "You realize this just turned the council chamber into a war zone."

"Good," I said. "They had it too quiet for too long."

That afternoon stretched like a long exhale after a storm. The café was closed, windows boarded, but the smell of smoke had started to fade. Sam brewed what was left of the beans, and for the first time in days, we sat without running.

Rangel arrived just before sunset. His jacket smelled faintly of smoke and exhaustion. "Grant's in custody. Trent's claiming he was just following orders. And the state's already asking questions about the Heritage Corridor fund."

Barlow nodded slowly. "Then it's done."

"Not exactly," Rangel said. "There's still missing money, and a few people who'll want payback. But you've made it impossible to bury." He looked at me. "You're not supposed to be the one solving these things, Calder."

"Then maybe Maplewood needs new job descriptions," I said.

He smiled despite himself. "Next time, try leading with a phone call instead of a fire."

"I'll add it to my list," I said.

When he left, the town was quiet again. Barlow lingered by the door, his eyes on the dark silhouette of the museum across the square.

"History always rebuilds," he said softly.

"Even if it has to start with ashes?" I asked.

"Especially then."

He turned to go, but paused. "If you ever tire of coffee," he said, "the museum will need curators when the dust settles."

I smiled. "Maybe I'll stick to mysteries."

"Then Maplewood's in capable hands," he said, and vanished into the evening fog.

That night, the clock tower struck eight, steady as breath. Beans jumped onto the counter beside me, tail flicking. Liam was fixing the espresso machine; Sam was closing the till. Outside, the square glowed under the streetlights—peaceful, for now.

I poured myself a small cup and watched the museum lights flicker through the haze. The town was quiet again, but I'd learned quiet in Maplewood was never permanent.

Somewhere deep down, I knew this wasn't over. Truth had a way of surfacing, just like smoke through cracks.

And in Maplewood, there were always more cracks waiting.

The bell over the door jingled once.

A stranger stepped inside, raincoat dripping, eyes scanning the café like he was checking for ghosts.

"Are you Hattie Calder?" he asked.

I set down my cup. "Who's asking?"

He held out a sealed envelope, water-stained but intact. "Dr. Barlow asked me to give you this."

Inside was a note, written in his precise, looping hand:

If you're reading this, I've gone where they can't find me. Keep looking. The medallion wasn't the only thing they hid. — F.B.

The words blurred slightly as the ink bled from a drop of rain.

I looked up. The stranger was already gone.

And somewhere outside, a single car engine started—slow, deliberate, familiar.

I smiled grimly and reached for my coat.

Maplewood wasn't finished talking yet.

The Man Who Vanished Twice

The rain started again that night, steady and deliberate, as if Maplewood itself was trying to rinse off the ashes. I locked the café early, the echo of Barlow's note still rolling through my head like a riddle that refused to sit still. The medallion wasn't the only thing they hid.
Liam leaned against the counter, laptop open, the faint glow of code reflected in his glasses. "You think he's in danger again?"
"I think he never stopped being," I said.
Sam dropped the mop into the bucket with a clatter. "You can't go chasing ghosts every time someone leaves a cryptic note."
"It's not a ghost if he's still bleeding ink," I said. "He's warning us. There's something left."
Liam looked up. "Maybe he means the second medallion. The twin."
"The what?" Sam asked.
He turned the screen toward us. A museum schematic filled the display. "The medallion that burned was catalogued as Silver Roast Medallion – Heritage Wing, accession number 1873-1. But look—there's an 1873-2 in the archive ledger. Same year, same description, listed as loaned, not displayed."
"Loaned to who?" I asked.
He zoomed in on the faded note at the bottom. "Unspecified private lender. No return date."
Sam frowned. "So there's another one floating around? And Barlow's note means he found out where?"
"Or that someone else did," I said.

By the time we left the café, the square was nearly empty except for the flashing red tape still strung across the museum entrance. The charred air carried that sharp tang of chemical burn. Maplewood's official calm had cracked again—reporters huddled under umbrellas, police lights still pulsed, and somewhere beyond it all, the truth was wriggling to the surface like a secret not ready to die.
Rangel's car sat half in shadow near the statue. He rolled the window down when he saw us. "You all look like people who aren't supposed to be out right now."
"We got a note," I said. "From Barlow."
He stared at me for a beat. "You're kidding."
I handed him the envelope. His jaw tightened as he read. "The man just vanished again, and you're telling me he left you homework?"

"I think it's more like a confession," I said.

He sighed, rubbing the bridge of his nose. "You realize the state's crawling over the museum right now? I've got two agencies arguing over jurisdiction and a mayor pretending he never heard of the Heritage Corridor."

"Then let us help," Liam said. "We might be able to trace the second medallion."

Rangel looked between us, then shook his head slowly. "You three are like a caffeine-fueled hydra. Cut off one lead, and two more pop up." He finally pocketed the note. "Alright. If there's a second medallion, it'll be tied to the ledger logs in the museum archive database. But that system's offline—fire damage."

Liam grinned faintly. "Offline doesn't mean unreachable."

Rangel sighed again. "Fine. If you're going to hack a crime scene, at least wait until after midnight. I'll clear the watch rotation for ten minutes. That's all I can do."

"Ten minutes is plenty," Liam said.

"Famous last words," Sam muttered.

The museum at night was different—quieter, hollowed out, a skeleton of its daytime charm. The fire had eaten the west wing clean, leaving the scent of wet ash and the gleam of standing water on marble floors. We slipped in through the side maintenance door Rangel had left unlatched, flashlights off, footsteps soft.

"Feels like walking through someone else's heartbeat," Liam whispered.

"Keep your poetic streak for later," I said. "Computer lab's this way."

We reached the admin offices. The walls were smoke-streaked but intact. Liam crouched beside the main console, prying open the casing with a screwdriver. Sparks flickered. "Burned connection, but the core's still good," he murmured. "If I bypass the main switch, I can ghost the data through my drive."

"English, please," Sam whispered.

"He's saying he can wake the dead," I said.

He grinned, fingers flying. "Exactly."

The screen blinked to life, lines of code racing across. A second later, the old museum logo appeared—half glitching, half alive. Liam navigated to the archives.

"There," he said. "Ledger entries, pre-2020. That's where the medallion data's stored."

The list scrolled endlessly. Barlow's careful handwriting had been scanned into the database years ago. Then Liam froze. "Got it."
He zoomed in. The second entry: Silver Roast Medallion II — loaned to Maplewood Historical Consortium, transferred under temporary custody to D. Grant, Council Archive Division.
Sam exhaled. "She took it."
"Not the museum's," I said. "The council's."
"And now she's in custody," Liam said. "So whoever she worked for still has it."
"Or wants it back," I said.
Before I could say more, a loud clatter echoed through the hall. We froze. Footsteps followed—the deliberate kind, too careful for first responders. Then a man's voice, low, confident: "I told you she'd come back."
I turned off the monitor light, but it was too late. Flashlight beams flooded the hall. The man from the bridge—the one in the dark coat—stood framed in the doorway.
He smiled without humor. "You kids really should learn when to quit."

The next few seconds moved too fast. Sam threw her flashlight into the corner; the man's beam instinctively followed it. Liam grabbed my arm, pulling me toward the emergency exit. We bolted down the corridor, boots splashing through puddles. The man shouted behind us, his voice calm and almost amused. "You can't hide what doesn't belong to you."
We hit the stairwell door. Liam jammed his screwdriver into the latch and twisted. The door jammed, sealing behind us with a loud metallic thud.
"That'll buy us a minute."
We ran down two flights until the stairs ended at the sub-basement level—the same one Barlow's map had marked weeks ago. A small red sign read ARCHIVAL STORAGE. The air was cold, damp, and thick with smoke.
"Wait," I said. "He didn't follow."
"Because he doesn't need to," Sam said. "We're running right where he wants us."
Liam looked around. "Then we make it count."
He flicked on his flashlight. The beam cut across rows of locked cabinets and waterlogged boxes. But one stood open—its door hanging crooked, its contents gone except for a small plaque nailed to the back wall.
Silver Roast Medallion II — Donated by the Barlow Estate.
Barlow's estate. My blood went cold.
"He knew," I said softly. "He hid it before any of this started."

"Which means," Liam said, "whoever burned the west wing was trying to find the first medallion to cover the second."

"Grant never stole it," Sam realized. "She was protecting it."

I shook my head. "Then why the recordings? Why the threats?"

"Because she wasn't protecting the truth," I said. "She was protecting herself."

A sound echoed down the stairs—slow, deliberate footsteps. The man's voice floated down the stairwell. "Thank you for finding my property."

Liam glanced at me. "Backup plan?"

"Same as always," I said. "Improvise."

We ducked behind the nearest row of cabinets as the footsteps reached the floor. The man moved slowly, flashlight beam sweeping the room. "You've done most of my work for me," he said. "Dr. Barlow was sentimental. Always thought he could choose which truths deserved to survive."

He stopped by the open cabinet. "But he kept the wrong one."

Liam's grip tightened on my sleeve. "He's got the case."

The man lifted a small black box from his coat and set it on the cabinet shelf. He pressed a code into the latch. The lid hissed open, releasing a faint metallic scent. Inside gleamed a twin to the original medallion—silver, intricate, alive with reflected light.

Sam whispered, "That's it."

The man smiled faintly. "You can come out now, Miss Calder."

I froze. "How do you know my name?"

"I make it my business to know anyone who gets too close to Maplewood's foundations," he said. "You've been an inconvenience. An admirable one. But this is where the story ends."

Something clicked behind him—metal meeting metal. Liam had crept up from the opposite aisle, holding one of the museum's fire extinguishers like a bat. "You should probably pick a less dramatic line next time," he said.

The man turned just as Liam swung. Foam exploded across the aisle, blinding him in a cloud of white. "Run!" I shouted.

We sprinted past him, up the stairs, through the emergency exit, and into the courtyard. Alarms blared again, echoing off the empty streets. Behind us, the man shouted something muffled, furious.

We didn't stop until we reached the square. My lungs burned; Sam doubled over, laughing from adrenaline. Liam clutched his bag like it was a lifeline.

"You got it?" I gasped.
He unzipped the pocket just enough to reveal the glint of silver inside.
"The medallion," he said. "He dropped it in the chaos."
I stared at it, heart pounding. "Barlow was right. They hid two."
Sam exhaled slowly. "Then what now?"
I looked at the dark silhouette of the museum, alarms still echoing through Maplewood. "Now," I said, "we find out why."
Because in Maplewood, every truth comes in pairs.
And sometimes, both of them burn.

Echoes in Silver

By dawn, Maplewood was pretending again. The news vans were gone, the tape around the museum had been replaced with polite "closed for safety inspection" signs, and the townsfolk shuffled past Brewed Awakening like nothing had ever burned. But beneath that practiced calm, I could feel it—the tremor of something waiting to crack again.
The medallion sat on our kitchen table wrapped in a napkin. Even through the cloth, it gleamed faintly, light catching on engraved letters I hadn't dared read yet.
Sam stared at it like it might bite. "We should've turned it in last night."
"To who?" I asked. "Grant's in custody, Rangel's stretched thin, and half the council's still pretending they didn't fund a land grab. You think evidence survives long in their hands?"
Liam rubbed his eyes. He hadn't slept. "It's got inscriptions on the back. I scanned it earlier—old Latin. Something like veritas sub cineres."
"Truth beneath the ashes," I translated. "Cute."
Sam frowned. "Barlow knew both medallions existed, didn't he? He didn't just hide this one—he meant for us to find it."
"Maybe," I said. "But the question isn't why he hid it. It's what it unlocks."

The café opened late that morning. Mabel Cho arrived the moment the lights flipped on, phone in hand, full of new gossip. "Council's gone silent," she whispered dramatically. "Half the files from last night's state inquiry disappeared before breakfast. Someone's scrubbing records again."
I poured her coffee. "And here I thought people would wait a full week before another cover-up."
She leaned in, lowering her voice. "Word is, the museum wasn't insured for the west wing. That's millions in renovations they'll have to explain."
Liam appeared from the back with his laptop. "Explain to who? Themselves?"
"Don't mock accountability," Mabel said, wagging a finger. "It's the Maplewood way to pretend we have it."
Sam ushered her toward a corner table before she could turn our morning into another breaking-news livestream. The moment the door closed behind her, I turned to Liam. "We need to see what's on that medallion."
He nodded. "I already started the analysis. There's a micro-etching layer under the engraving—barely visible without magnification."

"Meaning what?" Sam asked.
"Meaning this thing isn't just a relic. Someone modified it—recently."

We spent the next hour in the back office with Liam's improvised lab: a magnifier, a flashlight, and a lot of caffeine. He tilted the medallion under the light, revealing faint lines curling around the rim like circuitry etched into metal.
"There," he said, pointing. "That's not antique craftsmanship. That's modern. Nanopatterned metal."
"Like a code?" I asked.
"More like a data key," he said. "Barlow wasn't hiding treasure—he was hiding access."
"Access to what?" Sam said.
Liam smiled faintly. "Let's find out."
He scanned the medallion's surface with his phone's macro lens. The screen displayed the pattern in sharp relief. He ran it through an image parser he'd built during his "fun weekends," which apparently involved cracking old encryption puzzles for kicks.
The program beeped once, then displayed a string of coordinates and a single phrase: SUBSTRATUM ARCHIVE: ACCESS BY TWO.
"Coordinates," I said. "Riverbank?"
He nodded. "Just outside the old warehouse district—near the first tunnel entrance."
Sam folded her arms. "You're telling me a century-old medallion has GPS coordinates encoded on it?"
"I'm telling you," Liam said, "Barlow hid a modern access key inside an antique medallion. And this one leads somewhere."

We followed the coordinates just after dusk, when the town's noise dulled to a low hum and the air smelled of wet pavement and coffee grounds. The riverbank path was slick from the rain, the streetlights dim. Beyond the last row of warehouses, the dirt road narrowed into an overgrown service lane that led toward the water.
"Tell me again why we're following mystery coordinates in the dark," Sam said.
"Because daytime would make it too easy," I said.
Beans trotted beside us, tail high, as if he knew more than all of us combined.

The coordinates ended at a small metal shed half-buried in vines. A padlock hung open on the latch. Liam flicked on his flashlight, revealing rusted stairs spiraling down.
"Oh good," Sam muttered. "A creepy underground vault. My favorite genre."
I took the lead, the medallion cold in my pocket. The air grew cooler as we descended, the smell of river silt thickening. At the bottom, the stairwell opened into a narrow chamber—stone walls, a low ceiling, and a single steel door.
Etched above the door, barely legible, were the same words from the medallion: Veritas sub cineres.
Liam held up the medallion. "Think it's a key?"
"Only one way to find out," I said.
He pressed it against the indentation beside the lock. For a long second, nothing happened. Then a soft click echoed, followed by a faint mechanical whir. The door eased open.

The room beyond wasn't ancient at all. It looked like a small, secret archive—file cabinets lined the walls, stacked with labeled binders and sealed drives. Dust lay thick, but not untouched. Someone had been here recently.
Sam shone her flashlight across a plaque near the entry. "Substratum Archive — Maplewood Historical Consortium."
"Barlow's project," I whispered. "This is what he was protecting."
Liam opened the nearest drawer. Inside were manila folders stamped with the same council insignia we'd seen in the corridor. "These are the original museum grants," he said. "And look—ledger receipts from twenty years ago. Donor names, bank transfers, land contracts."
Sam flipped through one and froze. "Wait—look at this signature. Trent Morrow. Same as on the corridor deeds."
I scanned the other folder. "And here—Dolores Grant's initials. They weren't just funneling museum money—they were laundering private investments through fake preservation trusts."
Liam's voice was soft. "This is everything."
I nodded. "And the medallion was the only key."

Before we could celebrate, a sharp clatter echoed from the stairwell. I turned off my flashlight. Footsteps again—two pairs this time.
Liam whispered, "They followed us."
Sam's jaw tightened. "We should've known."

I reached for my phone, but a voice stopped me. Calm. Familiar. "Put the light down, Calder."

Rangel stepped into the doorway, gun drawn but pointed at the ground. Behind him, another silhouette—smaller, quicker. Councilman Trent Morrow.

Sam's voice cracked. "You're working with him?"

Rangel shook his head. "Not anymore."

Trent smirked. "Detective, you really should've picked a quieter time for betrayal."

Rangel ignored him. "Hattie, hand over the medallion."

I hesitated. "Whose side are you on?"

"The one that gets you all out of this alive," he said. "They're coming. Half the council, half the investors—they want what's in those files."

Trent laughed softly. "You think you can stop them? That thing in her pocket is worth more than Maplewood itself."

I looked between them—the tired detective, the smug councilman, the open archive humming quietly like it was holding its breath.

Then I tossed the medallion to Liam. "Run."

Liam bolted toward the back corridor, flashlight bouncing. Trent lunged, Rangel swung his arm, and the gun went off—one deafening crack that sent dust raining from the ceiling.

"Go!" Rangel shouted.

Sam grabbed my hand, pulling me toward the stairs. Behind us, Trent cursed, the sound of footsteps chasing. We scrambled upward into the cold night air.

When we finally burst through the shed door, the fog hit us like a wall. Liam was already ahead, clutching the medallion, breath visible in sharp bursts. "We can't lead them back to the café!"

"Then we go to the clock tower," I said. "If Barlow left a key, maybe he left a message."

Behind us, the sound of footsteps and engines grew louder.

Sam glanced back. "They won't stop, will they?"

"Not until the truth costs more than the lie," I said.

We ran.

Maplewood's river mist swallowed us whole, the medallion gleaming once in the beam of Liam's flashlight before vanishing again—like a secret refusing to die quietly.

The Tower Files

The fog clung to Maplewood like a secret that didn't want to be told. By the time we reached the clock tower, dawn had drained the sky to pale gray. The bells above us loomed silent, the brass gears hidden behind rusted panels that had ticked over centuries of gossip, politics, and small-town scandals. But right now, it felt less like a landmark and more like a refuge.

Liam reached the top first, slamming the heavy hatch behind us. He leaned against the wall, chest heaving, the medallion still clutched in his hand. "Please tell me we're not going to keep breaking into historically significant buildings forever."

"Depends how many secrets Maplewood's still hiding," I said.

Sam was already checking the windows. "No headlights on the hill yet. We bought a few minutes."

"Not enough," I said. "Rangel said half the council was coming."

Liam sank onto the dusty floor and held out the medallion. "Before we run again, maybe we should know what we're risking our lives for."

The clock tower's interior was all gears and ghosts. Old tools, half-finished repairs, forgotten notes scribbled by maintenance crews decades ago. But something about it felt… intentional. Like a place designed to keep watch.

I held up the medallion, turning it under the faint light from the window slats. The Latin inscription still shimmered— veritas sub cineres. But beneath it, I saw something else now that my eyes had adjusted: a faint engraving of the clock face itself, each Roman numeral etched with impossible precision.

"Look," I said. "It's not just decoration. The pattern's a code."

Liam squinted. "You think it points here?"

"Or something hidden here," I said.

Sam ran her hand along the railing, tracing her fingers over the metal. "If Barlow built this archive system to survive a purge, maybe he used landmarks. The medallion could be the first key—but the second…" She paused, glancing upward at the massive gears. "…might be the tower itself."

We climbed to the upper deck where the clock mechanism sat behind a pane of fogged glass. The bell above us creaked faintly, a sound that made the whole structure seem alive. Liam shone his flashlight through the gears.

"There," he said. "Behind the pendulum."

A small brass plate was bolted into the wall, nearly invisible under a layer of grime. Engraved into it were three words: Substratum Access Node.

Sam let out a low whistle. "He wasn't subtle."

Liam dug a screwdriver out of his pocket. "If the medallion fits that panel, I'll officially retire from ever mocking conspiracy theories."

"Don't you dare," I said.

He pressed the medallion into the circular groove beneath the inscription. It clicked perfectly into place.

For a moment, nothing happened. Then the gears above shifted, grinding faintly as a hidden compartment slid open beneath the main clock face. Inside was a small steel box, the kind used to store keys or old correspondence. Liam pulled it free and set it carefully on the floor.

Inside were three USB drives and a handwritten note.

Sam read it aloud. "'If this reaches you, Maplewood still matters. The medallions were never treasure. They were safeguards. Two halves of one archive—museum above, tower below. The truth was always split between power and memory.'"

Barlow's signature trailed off at the bottom.

"Two halves," I repeated. "So when the museum burned, this part survived."

Liam held up one of the drives. "Encrypted, obviously."

"Can you crack it?" Sam asked.

He smiled faintly. "Eventually. But we'll need power."

"We'll go back to the café," I said automatically, then froze. "No. They'll have it surrounded."

Sam nodded grimly. "Then where?"

"The old library," Liam said. "Still has grid power, and no one's checked it since the renovation got delayed. Plus…" he hesitated, glancing down the hill. "…it's where Barlow used to work before the museum."

Of course it was.

We packed the drives into a cloth bag and started down the narrow tower steps. The early light made the fog look like milk swirling through the streets below. Halfway down, Sam stopped, listening. A low rumble rose through the mist—engines, plural.

"They found us," she whispered.

Liam peered through a gap in the slats. "Black SUVs. Three of them. They're circling the square."

We ducked lower into the shadows, holding our breath as the vehicles parked below the tower. Doors opened. Boots on cobblestone. Then a voice—cold, sharp, familiar.

Trent Morrow.

"I told you," he called out. "They always come here first. The tower's the oldest safehouse in town. Check every floor."

"Terrific," Sam muttered. "He's read our script."

We exchanged a look. Then I whispered, "We can't go down. But there's another way."

The tower's north face had a maintenance ladder that led to the narrow bridge connecting to the library roof. It was a relic from when the two buildings shared wiring. Most people didn't even know it existed.

Liam eyed the gap. "You're kidding."

"Trust me," I said. "You're lighter than me. Go."

He grimaced but obeyed. One by one, we slipped through the narrow window and crawled onto the ladder, the wind biting our faces. The bridge creaked under our weight but held. Behind us, flashlights swept through the tower windows—searchers moving upward.

"Keep going," I whispered. "We're almost—"

The crack of gunfire split the morning.

A bullet sparked off the railing inches from Liam's hand. "They're shooting at us?" he shouted.

"Guess subtlety's dead," Sam hissed.

We scrambled the rest of the way across, ducking behind the parapet as more shots rang out. The library roof was half-collapsed from the last storm, but the skylight over the archives wing was still intact. I smashed it with the butt of my flashlight, clearing a path.

"Go!" I shouted.

We dropped through one by one, landing in a cloud of dust and shredded paper. The smell of old books and mildew was almost comforting.

Liam coughed. "Well, we're alive. Mostly."

Sam checked her phone. "No signal. But we've got power." She pointed to a humming junction box near the wall.

"Good," I said. "Let's see what's on those drives before Trent's cleanup crew decides to redecorate."

Liam connected the first drive. The laptop screen flickered to life, code scrolling. "Barlow's encryption isn't just password-locked—it's layered. Like a puzzle box."

"Can you open it?" Sam asked.

He grinned, that familiar spark of confidence cutting through the tension. "Eventually."

Minutes stretched. The hum of the old building mixed with the muffled voices outside as Trent's men spread through the square. Then, finally, a tone—a soft chime from the laptop.

The file opened.

On the screen was a collection of scanned documents, labeled simply: Project Revival — Phase II .

Sam leaned closer. "Phase Two of what?"

I scrolled through the text. My pulse quickened as the words came into focus.

"Maplewood Cultural Redevelopment Initiative... full demolition and reconstruction of designated historic zones... private investor consortium approval pending..."

"They were going to sell the entire town," I whispered. "Not just the museum."

Liam nodded grimly. "Barlow found out. That's why he split the archives. The medallions were meant to keep both halves of the plan separated. If one survived, so did the truth."

Sam's face was pale. "So Maplewood was never the project—it was the product."

Footsteps echoed in the library hallway.

"They're inside," Liam said, snapping the laptop shut.

I grabbed the bag of drives. "We take them and go."

"Where?" Sam asked.

"Anywhere but here."

We sprinted through the dusty aisles, weaving between toppled shelves. A voice echoed behind us—Trent again, furious now. "You think you can run forever? The truth doesn't save you, Calder—it isolates you!"

"Then I guess we'll be lonely," I called back.

We burst through the emergency door and into the sunlight. The mist was thinning, the town below waking up. Across the rooftops, sirens wailed—different ones this time. Police.

Liam looked back. "You called Rangel?"

I nodded. "Before we left the tower. He said, 'make it loud.'"

Sam grinned. "Oh, it's loud."

Behind us, Trent appeared at the door, wild-eyed. "You don't understand—this isn't over!"

I met his gaze. "Good," I said. "I'm not finished either."

We ran toward the clock tower as police cars swarmed the square, the sun breaking through at last—bright, merciless, and full of questions.

And in my pocket, the medallion gleamed again, warm this time, like it was waking up.

Maybe Maplewood finally was too.

Truth on the Clock

By the time the sun was fully up, Maplewood looked like a town under siege. The square teemed with flashing lights, police tape, and more reporters than residents. Rangel's officers fanned out across the cobblestones, corralling Trent's men one by one. The clock tower bells were silent, looming over the chaos like an impartial judge.
We ducked behind a vendor's cart as Rangel strode through the mess, barking orders. His coat was half buttoned, his coffee untouched, and his expression that particular blend of grim and furious that meant the truth had arrived earlier than his paperwork.
"Get those drives to evidence!" he shouted at one officer. "And keep Morrow separate from the others—he talks faster when he's cornered."
Sam peered over the edge of the cart. "He doesn't look mad at us."
Liam exhaled. "He's either grateful or too busy to yell. Let's not find out which."
I stepped out from cover. "Detective!"
Rangel turned. The sight of us made the vein at his temple twitch. "Of course you're here. Why wouldn't you be?"
"We have the drives," I said, holding up the cloth bag. "All of them."

He stared at the bag. "You mean to tell me you broke into a restricted building, stole classified evidence, ran across rooftops under gunfire, and somehow walked out with the most incriminating data cache in Maplewood history?"
"Yes," Sam said. "You're welcome."
He blinked. "I'm going to pretend you didn't say that. Give me the bag."
Liam hesitated. "Promise you won't let it vanish into a vault."
Rangel's jaw tightened. "You have my word. I'll make it public before the council tries to bury it."
I handed it over. "Barlow meant for it to surface. Just… not like this."
"Barlow meant well," Rangel said, "but his way got people killed. You three? You're lucky you're alive."
"Luck has good taste," Sam said.
Rangel didn't laugh. He looked past us, toward the museum ruins. "You realize what this means, right? The council's done. Grant, Morrow, half the donors—they're finished. The Heritage Corridor was a front for land laundering. And now every reporter in the state's got the story."
I followed his gaze. The museum's blackened skeleton gleamed in the sunlight like a confession.

"Then Maplewood's finally clean," I said.
Rangel snorted. "Clean? Calder, this is politics. Nothing's ever clean—just temporarily less dirty."

By late afternoon, the chaos had turned into ceremony. The state investigators arrived with clipboards and cautious optimism. Reporters crowded the police barricades, throwing questions that no one answered. Mabel Cho filmed everything from our café window, narrating with the authority of a true small-town correspondent.
Inside, Sam brewed the first calm cup of coffee I'd had in days. "Rangel says we're officially not under arrest," she said. "He also says if we ever pull something like this again, he'll personally revoke our caffeine privileges."
"Fair," I said. "He's earned it."
Liam sat at the bar, head resting on folded arms. "So we're done? Really done?"
"For now," I said. "Until Maplewood remembers it likes drama."
He lifted his head, eyes red from exhaustion. "Barlow's still missing."
"Maybe that's for the best," I said quietly. "He deserves peace."
Sam handed us each a mug. "To the museum," she said. "And to not dying."
We clinked our cups. Beans meowed like he wanted in on the toast.

Evening settled softly. The square quieted, replaced by the low hum of conversation and the clink of dismantled barricades. The smell of rain hung over everything. It should have felt like relief. It almost did.
I was wiping down the counter when the café door opened and a courier stepped in. "Delivery for Hattie Calder," he said, holding a padded envelope.
I frowned. "From who?"
He shrugged. "No return address. Just dropped off at the precinct."
I signed, slit the envelope open, and froze.
Inside was a single Polaroid. Grainy. Nighttime. The image showed the riverbank—the same one where we'd found the tunnel entrance. And standing near the water, half-lit by the reflection of the bridge lights, was Dr. Barlow.
Alive. Looking straight at the camera.
Scrawled on the back in his looping handwriting were five words:
"Truth sleeps where clocks forget."
Liam leaned over my shoulder. "That's... a riddle."

Sam groaned. "Oh no. No more riddles."

I stared at the photograph. The fog behind Barlow looked thicker than normal, like it was hiding something. The faint outline of a building loomed beyond him—an old boathouse, maybe. I'd walked that stretch a hundred times and never noticed it.

"He's pointing us somewhere," I said softly.

"Hattie," Sam warned. "Don't."

"He's alive," I said. "And he wants us to find something."

Liam squinted at the photo. "The clocks. The tower? Or time itself?"

"Or both," I murmured. "He said truth sleeps where clocks forget. Maybe he means a place that time forgot."

"Which would be…" Sam crossed her arms. "Let me guess. The old river foundry."

I looked up. "Exactly."

By the time we closed the café, the square was quiet again. The last patrol car rolled past, headlights glinting off the rain-wet cobblestones. Rangel had gone home to draft statements and manage reporters. Maplewood, as usual, was pretending everything was fine.

But as I locked the door, the medallion in my pocket felt heavier. Warmer. Almost alive.

Liam looked at me. "We're really going to follow that clue, aren't we?"

"Of course we are," I said.

Sam sighed, pulling on her coat. "I was afraid you'd say that."

The three of us stepped into the fog, the café lights fading behind us. Somewhere across the square, the clock tower struck ten—slow, deliberate, echoing through the mist.

Each chime felt like a heartbeat.

And I couldn't shake the feeling that Maplewood was still counting down.

Where Clocks Forget

The foundry sat on the edge of town, swallowed by vines and years. Its iron bones jutted out from the riverbank like the ribs of some industrial ghost. The closer we got, the more it felt like the air itself thickened, carrying that faint metallic scent of rust and rain-soaked history. The place had been closed since before I was born. The sign on the fence still read: Maplewood Foundry — Since 1894, the "Since" hanging crookedly like it had given up on time altogether.
"This is where clocks forget," Liam murmured, adjusting his flashlight.
Sam eyed the dark expanse ahead of us. "This is also where people disappear in every horror movie ever made."
I smiled faintly. "Then it's good we brought our own plot armor."
She didn't laugh. Beans, perched on the fence post, flicked his tail and stared into the fog like he was waiting for something. Maybe he was. He'd led us to the right places before.
We ducked under the broken section of fencing and stepped inside.

The foundry floor was a graveyard of machinery. Hulking silhouettes of rusted presses and cranes loomed in the shadows, their shapes barely visible under the thin wash of moonlight that filtered through broken panes. Puddles mirrored the old beams, and the steady drip of water echoed through the vast space like a ticking clock.
Liam's light caught on a trail of footprints in the dust. "Someone's been here recently."
"Barlow," I said. "Has to be."
"Or someone following him," Sam countered.
We moved carefully, the sound of our steps small against the vast stillness. The trail led to the far end of the building where a series of rusted lockers leaned against the wall. One was half open, its door bent inward. Inside sat an old thermos, a notebook, and something wrapped in oilcloth.
Liam peeled the cloth away, revealing a small metal cylinder with a data port at the top. "A drive container," he said. "Industrial-grade. Fireproof, waterproof, and encrypted."
"Barlow's last cache," I said softly. "He wanted it to outlive him."
Sam flipped through the notebook. "Coordinates, dates, council initials... Hattie, look at this. These go back twenty years."

Liam powered on his tablet, connecting the cylinder with a cable. The screen flickered. A single file appeared, titled SUBSTRATUM — CLOSURE PROTOCOL.
He opened it.

Barlow's voice filled the air, recorded but sharp and steady.
"If you're hearing this, it means Maplewood's truth has woken again. The medallions were never about treasure—they were keys to separation. Power divided is harder to corrupt. But I misjudged the players. Grant saw opportunity; Morrow saw profit. And I... I saw ghosts."
A pause. Papers shuffled. Then his voice again, softer this time.
"The Substratum Project was designed to preserve Maplewood's cultural identity against commercial erasure. Every file, every record, every voice mattered. Until they decided it was easier to rewrite history. They didn't just want the land—they wanted the narrative. But history doesn't burn easily."
The recording crackled. "To whoever finds this: the council's corruption isn't the root—it's the symptom. The real infection started higher. Follow the funding, and you'll find the Consortium."
Then static. Then silence.
Liam leaned back slowly. "Consortium?"
Sam frowned. "As in...?"
"The Maplewood Historical Consortium," I said. "It was on the medallion. On the archive room plaque."
"Except it's not a non-profit, is it?" Liam said quietly. "It's the shell company. The one pulling the strings."

A faint sound cut through the quiet—a door creaking open somewhere behind us. We froze. The light from Liam's tablet flickered across the wall.
Footsteps. Slow. Careful. Someone else was here.
I mouthed, Hide.
We ducked behind one of the old presses. Through the narrow gaps in the rusted frame, I saw a figure moving through the foundry. A man in a long coat, flashlight beam sweeping the floor. He stopped near the lockers, crouched, and picked up the oilcloth we'd dropped.
Then he spoke, low and even.
"You're getting predictable, Calder."
Trent Morrow.
Liam clenched his jaw. "How does he keep finding us?"

"He doesn't," I whispered. "He's being sent."
Sam leaned close. "You think the Consortium—"
"Uses him as cleanup? Absolutely."
Trent straightened, scanning the shadows. "You should've taken Rangel's deal," he said. "You could've walked away. Instead, you keep digging."
I stepped out before Sam could stop me. "Maybe that's because digging's the only thing that works around liars."
His flashlight beam found my face. He smiled without warmth. "You think this is about a town? About property lines? The Consortium owns half the state, Calder. Maplewood's just where the ledger started."
Liam stepped out beside me. "And where it's going to end."
Trent shook his head. "You don't even understand what you've opened."
I held up the cylinder. "I think this says otherwise."
His smile vanished. "Give it to me."
"Not a chance."
He took one step closer—and Beans, from somewhere above, let out a sharp yowl. Something small and metallic tumbled from the rafters, landing at Trent's feet with a clatter.
An old wrench.
He looked up—just as I threw the nearest thing I could reach: a coffee thermos. It hit his flashlight hand dead-on. The light went spinning, the beam dancing across the walls.
"Run!" I shouted.

We sprinted toward the far door, our footsteps thundering across the metal floor. Trent's voice echoed behind us. "You can't save a town that sold itself decades ago!"
Liam shoved the door open, and we burst into the cold night air. The river stretched before us, wide and silver in the moonlight. Sam glanced back. "He's coming!"
We ran along the bank toward the bridge. Halfway there, I stopped.
"Wait—if we lead him to town, he'll draw them right to Rangel."
"Then what do we do?" Liam panted.
I held up the cylinder. "We make sure this survives."
Sam's eyes widened. "No. You're not—"
But I was already at the edge of the pier. I took a deep breath, twisted the cylinder's release cap, and dropped it into the river. It vanished with barely a splash.
Liam stared at me. "You just—"

"It's waterproof, remember? Barlow designed it to outlive fire. Now it just has to outlive them."

Trent burst out of the foundry behind us, shouting. But by the time he reached the riverbank, we were gone—vanished into the fog.

We didn't stop running until the bridge lights came into view again. My lungs burned, my pulse roared, and every part of me screamed that this wasn't over. Because it wasn't.

Sam slowed beside me. "You realize what you just did?"

"Saved us a target," I said. "If Trent can't find the file, he has to chase ghosts instead."

Liam managed a laugh between breaths. "So now the truth's buried. Literally."

"Exactly where it belongs," I said. "For now."

We stood there for a long moment, watching the river swirl beneath the bridge. Somewhere below, Barlow's voice and Maplewood's last unburned secret waited in the dark.

And if his clue was right, that's where we'd have to go next.

Because the truth might sleep where clocks forget—

—but Maplewood never really sleeps at all.

The River Knows

The next morning, Maplewood was almost too quiet—like the air was waiting for someone to breathe first. The fire trucks were gone, the police tape fluttered in the breeze, and the clock tower's bells stood still. Even the pigeons seemed to have taken the day off. It would've looked peaceful if you didn't know what was lurking beneath the river.

Liam stirred his coffee at the counter, eyes on the tablet he'd set to monitor local networks. "Trent's name is everywhere. Rangel's making it public—embezzlement, obstruction, corporate fraud. He's blaming the Consortium for everything."

Sam looked up from the register. "Doesn't that mean we won?"

I shook my head. "No. It means they just went quiet."

Because that's what power does when it's cornered—it doesn't vanish; it burrows deeper.

Liam frowned at the screen. "There's something else. Late-night shipping records from the Maplewood port authority. Unauthorized barge departure at 2:37 a.m.—destination redacted. Cargo listed as 'metal waste and archive salvage.'"

Sam's mug froze halfway to her lips. "Archive salvage. You don't think—"

"I do," I said. "They're dredging the river."

Liam glanced up. "Then they found the cache."

"Or they're looking for it," I said. "Either way, we can't let them pull it out first."

The river was a silver-gray stretch of silence when we reached it, fog hanging low over the water like smoke that had forgotten what to burn. A work barge idled near the bridge, two men in reflective vests loading a crane rig with thick cables. The sound of engines rumbled faintly against the current.

"They're not city contractors," Liam whispered. "Wrong uniforms."

Sam squinted through the mist. "Private salvage crew?"

"Private muscle," I said. "Consortium money."

We crouched behind a cluster of reeds, the mud sucking at our boots. I could see one of the men operating a scanner—industrial-grade sonar. The other man barked coordinates into a headset.

"They know something's down there," Liam murmured. "They're mapping the riverbed."

"And if they get it first, they'll bury it again," I said.

Sam rubbed her forehead. "What's your plan this time? Don't say 'wing it.'"

I smiled faintly. "Fine. Improvised coordination with flair."

"Otherwise known as winging it," she muttered.

We waited until one of the men stepped away from the crane to take a phone call. The second was busy adjusting the sonar feed. Liam slipped around the barge's blind side, crouched low, and unplugged the portable console from its mount.

"Thirty seconds before they notice," he whispered through the comm mic clipped to his collar.

I ran along the pier to the control shack. A single technician was inside, radio pressed to his ear. He looked up just as I pushed the door open.

"Hey!" he barked. "You can't—"

"Maintenance check," I said, and before he could argue, Sam swung the door shut behind me and locked it. The man lunged for the radio, but Liam's voice cut in over the comm: "Signal's jammed. Two minutes."

We tied the tech's hands with an extension cord and stepped back onto the dock.

"Liam, you've got control?" I asked.

"Mostly," he said. "I rerouted the scanner feed. The sonar thinks the cache is fifty meters upriver."

"And when they drop the crane there?" Sam asked.

"They'll be fishing for ghosts," I said. "Meanwhile, we dive where it actually is."

Sam blinked. "Dive?"

I pointed to the small maintenance skiff tied to the dock. "We need to get the cylinder first."

Liam stared at the murky water. "Please tell me you have a better idea."

I grinned. "Not today."

The water was colder than I'd expected, dark as ink and twice as heavy. Every sound dulled beneath the surface—the hum of the barge, the creak of the crane, even my own heartbeat. Liam swam beside me, flashlight strapped to his wrist, his expression halfway between focus and panic.

"Remind me," he said through the comm mic, "how we keep ending up in rivers?"

"Because Maplewood likes metaphors," I replied.

We followed the current to where I'd dropped the cylinder. The riverbed was silt and stone, littered with old scrap metal. I swept my light across the floor until a glint caught my eye—silver against the dark.
"There," I said. "Half-buried."
We dug it free, the mud sucking at it like a secret that didn't want to be told. The cylinder was intact, cold to the touch, its LED still blinking faintly. Liam whooped into his mic. "It's alive!"
"Not yet," I said. "Let's get it out before they realize we're not part of the crew."
We kicked upward, breaking the surface just as the crane above us groaned and lowered a magnet into the false coordinates upriver. The salvage men shouted to each other, none of them looking our way.
Sam waved from the skiff. "You've got it?"
Liam tossed the cylinder aboard. "You bet."
"Then let's make like bad tourists," I said.
We pushed off from the dock, the motor purring quietly as the skiff drifted downriver with the fog. Behind us, the crane slammed into the mud with a hollow clang, pulling up nothing but rusted debris.
"Enjoy your ghosts," I muttered.

Back at the café, we locked the door and cleared the counter. Liam hooked the cylinder to his laptop. The screen flickered, codes racing faster than before. A progress bar appeared—Decrypting: 12%.
Sam poured coffee for all three of us. "So this is it. The last piece."
"Until the next mystery shows up," I said.
Liam smirked. "You say that like it's a bad thing."
The percentage climbed—48%, 73%, 100%. The screen went black for a heartbeat, then filled with folders. Each one stamped with a different name.
Sam read the first aloud. "Consortium Holdings. State Investments. Federal Cultural Board."
"These are contracts," Liam said. "They weren't just laundering land—they were trading influence. Museum boards, universities, preservation grants—it's all tied together."
I scrolled down to the bottom. The final file was labeled: Founders Agreement — Signatories.
When I opened it, three names appeared.
Dolores Grant.
Trent Morrow.
Frederick Barlow.

The air went still.
Sam whispered, "He was part of it."
Liam shook his head. "That can't be right. He tried to stop them."
"Maybe he built the system before he realized what it would become," I said. "Maybe that's why he ran."
Sam set her mug down hard. "So the man we've been protecting was the architect of the corruption?"
I met her gaze. "Maybe he was the one trying to fix it from the inside."
Liam leaned back. "Or maybe both."

The laptop chimed. A new message appeared on the screen—timestamped just one hour ago. No sender.
It read: If you want the whole truth, come alone. River foundry. Midnight.
Below it, a signature: F.B.
Sam swore under her breath. "He's alive."
Liam looked at me, eyes wide. "You're not seriously going."
"Of course I am," I said.
"Hattie—"
"If he's the architect, I need to hear him say it. If he's the whistleblower, I need to know what comes next."
Sam crossed her arms. "You won't go alone."
"I have to," I said. "If it's a trap, you two stay clear."
Liam frowned. "And if it's not?"
"Then Maplewood finally gets to hear the truth from the man who built the lie."

The clock tower struck eleven as I left the café. The fog was back, thicker than before, swallowing sound. I walked down the silent streets toward the river, every step echoing like it already belonged to memory.
Maplewood was quiet again—but I knew better. The river had its own voice now.
And tonight, it was going to talk.

The Confession in the Fog

The river looked different at midnight. Blacker, quieter, deeper. The fog pressed low over the water, muting every sound except the slow lap of current against the pier. The foundry's silhouette rose from the mist ahead, half-ruined and glinting faintly in the moonlight. A single light burned inside—small, flickering, like someone was waiting for me. Barlow's message hadn't included coordinates, but I didn't need them. The river remembered the way.
I slipped through the fence gap, my boots sinking into the damp earth. The air smelled of oil and rust and something older—like time itself was corroding.
"Dr. Barlow?" I called softly.
No answer.
The light swayed once. Lantern. Manual. A human signal.
I moved closer, one hand on the pocketed medallion. The foundry door creaked open before I touched it.
Barlow stood in the doorway.
He looked smaller somehow—paler, thinner, like the fog had been eating at him. His face was tired, eyes bloodshot, but when he smiled, it was the same kind one gives a student who finally solved a puzzle.
"I knew you'd come," he said.
"I wasn't sure you'd still be alive."
"Neither was I," he said. "Come in, Hattie."

The foundry's interior glowed with the weak light of a single lantern on a crate. Around it were maps, folders, and a tangle of old equipment—the same kind we'd found in the archive tunnels. The air shimmered with faint heat from a small generator humming in the corner.
"You sent us on a chase," I said. "You faked your disappearance, let everyone think you were dead. Why?"
He sank onto a crate and rubbed his hands together. "Because the truth had to survive longer than I could."
I crossed my arms. "Then start talking."
He nodded slowly. "The Consortium began as preservation. We were historians, curators, idealists. But money stains everything it touches. The council offered funding—development grants, restoration projects, political sponsorships. At first it was about saving the town's history. Then it became about rewriting it."

"And you helped them," I said. "Your name's on the Founder's Agreement."

His eyes closed for a moment. "Yes. I built the Substratum system. I wanted to preserve Maplewood's records digitally—to make them impossible to destroy. But Trent and Grant realized what I hadn't: control of the archive meant control of the narrative. They twisted it. Used the medallions as encryption keys to lock out oversight."

"And when you found out?"

He gave a soft, bitter laugh. "I tried to expose them. But by then, the files were already split between two medallions. I couldn't unlock both without help. Grant had one. I hid the other in the museum vault. Then the fires started."

"You should've told someone."

"I did," he said quietly. "I told Owen Pike. And they killed him for it."

The weight of that name hit like cold water. Owen—our first casualty, the assistant everyone thought had simply gone missing after the gala.

"So the recording… the fires… the river cache. All of it was to force exposure?"

He nodded. "I knew I couldn't fight them head-on. But I could build a breadcrumb trail for someone who might. Someone who wouldn't give up when the story got ugly."

I stared at him. "You mean me."

"I mean anyone with enough stubbornness to care," he said softly. "You just happened to fit."

The generator flickered. The shadows seemed to shift around us. Barlow glanced toward the door. "We don't have much time. They'll come."

"Trent's in custody."

"Trent's a pawn," he said. "You still don't understand what the Consortium is. Maplewood's just their experiment—a small town used to test large-scale narrative control. Real estate, heritage, education, tourism—it's all the same currency. Rewrite what people believe, and you own what they build."

He opened a folder and slid it across the crate toward me. Inside were printed emails, contracts, and transfer ledgers. "These are the original agreements—the ones never digitized. They show how the Consortium expanded beyond Maplewood. If they're made public, this doesn't end in one town—it exposes an entire system."

"And why me again?" I asked. "Why not Rangel? Why not the press?"

"Because you don't have a side to lose," he said. "You care about the truth more than the headline."
The words should've felt flattering. They didn't. They felt like pressure.
"So what now?" I asked.
Barlow looked toward the river. "Now, we finish what we started."
He lifted the medallion from around his neck—the twin to mine—and held it out. "Together, they complete the sequence. The final unlock."
I hesitated, then handed him mine. The two medallions clicked together like gears finding their rhythm. His lantern flickered as the generator's hum deepened. The air thickened with a faint metallic vibration.
Barlow set the combined medallion onto a small reader connected to his laptop. Code spilled across the screen like a storm of numbers.
"Final authentication," he whispered. "Truth beneath the ashes."

A soft tone chimed. Then the screen filled with lines of text—an automated upload. Every document, every recording, every hidden ledger from the Substratum archive copied itself to a secure public domain server.
I watched, speechless.
"It's irreversible," Barlow said. "No one can bury it now. Not the Consortium, not the council, not me."
Then a voice echoed from the doorway. "You sure about that?"
We both turned.
Trent stood framed in the light of a new lantern, his coat wet from the rain, a pistol steady in his hand.
"I told you," he said, eyes locked on Barlow. "You don't understand what you've unleashed."
Barlow's jaw clenched. "You can't stop it now. It's already transmitting."
Trent stepped closer. "You think the Consortium cares about files? They care about leverage. And right now, I have all of it."
The generator buzzed louder. The fog outside thickened, curling into the foundry through the open door. I could barely see Trent's face, only the faint gleam of the gun.
"Move away from the computer," he said.
"No," I said.
He sighed. "Then this ends messy."
The sound of a safety clicking off echoed sharp as glass.
Then, from somewhere behind him, another voice—calm, deliberate.
"Drop it, Morrow."

Rangel stepped from the shadows, gun drawn, badge glinting in the lantern light. "Hands up."
Trent froze. His jaw twitched. "You're too late."
"Try me," Rangel said.
The tension snapped all at once. Trent turned, firing. Rangel dove. The shot went wide, hitting the generator. Sparks flew, the hum turning into a scream of metal. I lunged forward, knocking the laptop off the crate just as the generator blew.
The blast was deafening. Light and heat surged through the foundry. The shock threw me backward. When I opened my eyes, smoke filled the room and the air was thick with the smell of burning wire.
Barlow was gone.
So was Trent.
Only the medallions remained, fused together, still glowing faintly where they'd landed among the ashes.

Rangel staggered to his feet, coughing. "You alive?"
"Mostly," I said. "Barlow—"
He shook his head. "Gone. The river took him."
"And Trent?"
"Same."
We stood there in the flickering ruin, the fog curling through the open doorway like it was reclaiming its own. The laptop lay cracked, the upload frozen on its final line.
TRANSFER COMPLETE.
Rangel looked at me. "It's out, Calder. Whatever this was—it's finished."
I stared at the medallions. "No," I said softly. "It's started."

By morning, the story broke worldwide. Cultural Consortium Corruption Scandal filled every news feed. Maplewood became the headline town of the week—half proud, half infamous. The truth had finally surfaced, but the cost was higher than any of us had guessed.
At Brewed Awakening, Sam and Liam watched the news from the counter, mugs untouched. Rangel stopped by once, silent but with that same exhausted relief that looked too much like guilt.
And me? I still couldn't stop hearing Barlow's last words.
Truth beneath the ashes.
The foundry still smoked three days later. The river ran darker near its edge. And somewhere beneath it, the man who'd started everything was finally quiet.

But I had the medallions—what was left of them—and I wasn't sure the story was over.
Because if Maplewood had taught me anything, it was that secrets don't drown.
They wait.

The Quiet After the Storm

The next few days blurred into headlines and half-slept nights. Maplewood, once a quiet coffee-scented postcard, had become the epicenter of a national storm. Every screen, every paper, every whisper carried the same story: The Maplewood Files Expose Nationwide Cultural Corruption.
But behind the reporters and applause, the town itself looked hollow—like truth had taken too much with it when it surfaced.
Brewed Awakening reopened with cracked windows and new locks. Sam insisted it was "for morale," though I suspected she needed the smell of coffee and conversation to drown out everything else. Liam fixed the shop's Wi-Fi, patched the backdoor firewall, and started teaching himself to sleep again.
Rangel stopped by daily now. He never said much—just ordered black coffee, left his badge face down on the counter, and read the newspaper like it still held something he didn't already know.
And me? I couldn't stop hearing the river.

On the fifth morning after the explosion, a package arrived. No sender. No return address.
Sam brought it into the backroom like it might be ticking. "If this thing starts smoking, I'm tossing it in the grinder."
I cut the twine carefully. Inside was a small wooden box, hand-carved, smelling faintly of cedar and machine oil.
Nestled inside the velvet lining was a single item.
A pocket watch.
Old, but well-kept—its glass scratched, its hands frozen at 12:37.
And on its back, engraved in careful script:
"Where clocks forget, time remembers." — F.B.
Liam leaned over my shoulder. "Barlow."
Sam exhaled. "He's supposed to be dead."
"Supposed to be," I echoed.
The watch clicked faintly when I turned it over, like something inside still wanted to run.
Tucked beneath it was a note, scrawled in Barlow's precise handwriting:
There are still names missing from the list. The Consortium wasn't just ours. If you follow the ledger's trail beyond the state lines, you'll find the next archive. They're already rebuilding. Trust the clock—it knows where the next one sleeps.

Liam read it twice. "So he's alive."
"Or he planned for this," Sam said.
"Both," I whispered.

That night, I sat on the café balcony above the square, the clock tower bells ticking softly behind me. The pocket watch sat beside my coffee cup, unmoving but heavy, like it carried gravity instead of gears.
Below, Maplewood tried its best to feel normal again. Couples strolled. Cars passed. Mrs. Pickles was hosting a candlelit vigil for "the dearly departed historical ghosts." Mabel Cho was live-streaming it.
But even through the laughter and the clinking cups, I could feel it: an undercurrent, faint but steady. The truth we'd exposed hadn't destroyed the town—it had changed it. Every conversation felt more cautious now, every smile edged with questions.
Rangel joined me quietly, leaning against the railing. He didn't need an invitation.
"You got the watch," he said.
"You knew it would come?"
He nodded. "Barlow left me one too. Mine's still ticking."
"Does it say anything?"
He smiled faintly. "Just a note: 'Keep her alive long enough to finish it.' I assume he meant you, not the town."
"I'm touched," I said dryly. "You think he's still out there?"
"Men like Barlow don't die easy," Rangel said. "They just find quieter corners."
He sipped his coffee. "You realize this isn't over, right? The state wants your testimony. The Bureau's asking for access to the drives. And there are people—powerful people—who aren't thrilled about what you uncovered."
"Let them be unthrilled," I said. "Truth doesn't expire."
He smiled. "I'll quote you on that."
We watched the river shimmer under the streetlights. The fog was gone tonight, replaced by a sharp, clean chill that made everything feel new.
Finally, Rangel set his cup down. "Whatever happens next, Calder… stay grounded. Don't let the mystery eat you."
"Coming from you, that's rich," I said.
He chuckled and headed down the stairs. "See you at sunrise. And lock the door this time."

After he left, I picked up the watch again. Its weight felt familiar, like the medallion's echo—part memory, part warning.

I wound it once, gently.

The second hand twitched. Then began to move.

Tick.

Tick.

Tick.

And somewhere in the distance, the clock tower bells answered—twelve slow chimes, clear and steady, rolling across the quiet town like a promise.

When the last note faded, I slipped the watch into my coat pocket and smiled.

"Guess we're not done, Barlow," I whispered. "Not even close."

Below, the river rippled once, catching the moonlight like a wink.

The town had its truth now.

And Maplewood's secrets, like time itself, were still ticking.

Brewed Awakening

Two weeks after the explosion, the town finally started pretending to breathe again. Brewed Awakening was half full every morning, its chatter cautious but hopeful—like everyone had agreed to rebuild the town's rhythm one cup at a time.

Sam added a new drink to the menu: the Fog Breaker Latte. Liam swore it tasted like redemption; I said it tasted like burnt sugar and insomnia. Either way, it was selling faster than we could steam milk.

The café had become the unofficial headquarters for every discussion about "the future of Maplewood." City planners, reporters, students—they all came here, as if our tiny espresso machine had turned into the town's moral compass.

I'd tried to stay out of it. But Maplewood had a way of dragging me back in.

That morning, Rangel came in early, looking like he hadn't slept.
"They're calling it a partial victory," he said, sliding into the stool beside the register.
"Partial?" I asked.
"The Bureau shut down three branches of the Consortium. But the upper structure vanished—offshore accounts, empty buildings, no names. It's like the top tier evaporated overnight."
Sam poured him a cup. "People with power don't vanish," she said. "They relocate."
Rangel nodded grimly. "And if Barlow's alive, they'll find him first."
I leaned against the counter. "Maybe that's why he sent the watch."
Rangel's eyes flicked to my pocket. "Still ticking?"
I nodded. "Always."
He exhaled. "Good. Because I have a feeling you're going to need it."
Before I could ask, Liam came rushing from the back with his tablet.
"Hey, I found something."
"Please tell me it's good," Sam muttered.
"That depends on how you define good," Liam said. "Remember the encrypted data from the Consortium drive? There's a new IP pinging the file mirror every twelve hours. It's not government. It's not public. It's private, routed through three dummy servers in Eastern Europe."
Rangel frowned. "You saying someone's still accessing the archive?"
Liam nodded. "Not accessing. Expanding. Someone's adding files."

We huddled around his screen. Dozens of new document names scrolled across the mirrored database: small towns, museums, heritage centers, each tagged with a date and an archive code.
"Wait," Sam said. "Those look like... new Substratum nodes."
"Exactly," Liam said. "Someone's rebuilding the network."
Rangel rubbed his temples. "They're already back online. Two weeks. That's all it took."
I stared at the list. "It's not just Maplewood anymore. It's spreading."
Sam looked between us. "So what do we do? Blow up another archive?"
"No," I said slowly. "We find who's behind it before they finish."
Liam looked pale. "That could be anywhere. Any country. We'd need access to their backend system, global routing data—"
"Which you can do," I said.
He blinked. "I was afraid you'd say that."
Rangel stood. "If you're going after them, I'll need official cause. Something more than curiosity and caffeine."
I grinned faintly. "Then make it about preservation."
He raised an eyebrow. "Preservation?"
"Yeah," I said. "If they're rewriting history again, we're just protecting it. That's what curators do."

The plan came together in fragments over the next few days—late nights at the café, quiet meetings in the tower, encrypted messages sent through Liam's improvised relay system.
We started small: verifying which nodes were real, which were decoys. Most of the new Substratum sites were linked to cultural councils or private archives—places with no idea they were part of a reconstruction project.
But one name kept resurfacing.
The Verity Foundation.
Sam frowned when she read it. "Sounds like a front."
Liam checked the domain registry. "Founded six months ago. Headquarters listed as 'Athens Restoration Initiative.' But the contact info routes through an old museum consortium in Chicago."
Rangel's voice dropped. "And the registered founder?"
He turned his screen toward us.
Frederick Barlow.
My stomach sank. "No."
"Looks like he didn't just survive," Liam said quietly. "He went global."

We sat in silence for a long moment, the hum of the espresso machine the only sound between us.
Finally, Sam spoke. "So either he's the hero who took the fight bigger…"
"Or the architect who started over," I finished.
Rangel crossed his arms. "Both could be true."
Liam scrolled further. "Look at this. Their public statement: 'Restoring truth to forgotten histories.' Sounds noble enough."
"Yeah," I said. "So did the last one."

That night, I walked the river again. The fog had returned, thicker this time, crawling over the water like memory. The pocket watch ticked quietly in my coat.
When I reached the bridge, I stopped. The clock tower glowed faintly behind me, steady, patient, eternal. I opened the watch.
It was still frozen at 12:37.
But the second hand trembled—just once—like it wanted to move but wasn't ready.
I looked down at the reflection on the river's surface and whispered, "If you're still out there, Barlow, tell me what you're doing."
The fog shifted. A figure crossed the far bank—too distant to see, but familiar in posture. A man in a coat, lantern in hand.
He paused, turned toward me, and raised the light once in silent acknowledgment.
Then he disappeared into the mist.
The watch ticked again.
Just once.
And stopped.

By morning, I knew what we had to do.
Brewed Awakening had been our refuge, but Maplewood wasn't where the story ended. The Verity Foundation had to be traced—root to root, archive to archive—before it rewrote more than just one town's history.
I slipped the pocket watch into my bag beside the fused medallions. Liam was already prepping the network tools. Sam was packing travel mugs. Rangel had filed a "consultation request" with his superiors for "interstate cultural investigation."
Before we left, I flipped the café's open sign one last time and looked out at the square.
The fog was lifting. The town looked cleaner, brighter. But under that, I could still feel it—quiet, stubborn, patient.

Maplewood's heartbeat.
And somewhere out there, so was his.

The clock tower chimed nine times as we pulled out of town, our little car loaded with laptops, maps, and too much hope.
The sound echoed through the valley—slow, deliberate, and alive.
As we crossed the bridge, Liam glanced back at the reflection of the tower in the river. "You think we'll ever come back?"
"Maybe," I said. "But right now, the story's still moving."
He smiled. "Like time?"
"Exactly," I said. "And it's our turn to keep it ticking."
The watch in my pocket ticked once more—steady, certain, and very much awake.

Made in United States
Troutdale, OR
02/09/2026